No matter how dar... ...faces, Rachel knows s... ...tions she used in her p...

The old Rachel might have ... ...her parents, explained Jimmy's demands, and begged them to come up with the money. The old Rachel might have gone to Adam and promised him anything to help her. She abhorred the thoughts of the woman she once was, the despicable person who schemed and manipulated others to obtain those things she wanted.

The new Rachel, the one who gave her life to Jesus, trusted Him to show her what to do. She believed with all her heart that Jimmy could be stopped, and she'd find a way—a way not involving illegal or immoral maneuvers.

Lord, I trust You to guide me through this horrible mess. I pray for the safety of my children, my parents, Adam, and Bud. Shelter me from taking any action that does not honor You.

Clutching the door to the restaurant, she swallowed the bile rising in her throat. She dared not tell anyone about Jimmy's demands until she could think more clearly. She willed herself not to grow pale, be distracted. Evil would not triumph over good.

DIANN MILLS lives in Houston, Texas, with her husband, Dean. They have four adult sons. She wrote from the time she could hold a pencil, but not seriously until God made it clear that she should write for Him. After three years of serious writing, her first book *Rehoboth* won favorite **Heartsong Presents** historical for 1998. Other publishing credits include magazine articles and short stories, devotionals, poetry, and internal writing for her church. She is an active church choir member, leads a ladies' Bible study, and is a church librarian.

Books by DiAnn Mills

HEARTSONG PRESENTS
HP291—Rehoboth
HP322—Country Charm
HP374—The Last Cotillion
HP394—Equestrian Charm
HP410—The Color of Love
HP441—Cassidy's Charm
HP450—Love in Pursuit
HP504—Mail-Order Husband
HP527—The Turncoat
HP572—Temporary Husband

Compassion's Charm

DiAnn Mills

Heartsong Presents

*To Ben and Julie Egert for your compassion
and your love toward others.*

A note from the Author:
*I love to hear from my readers! You may correspond with me
by writing:*

**DiAnn Mills
Author Relations
PO Box 719
Uhrichsville, OH 44683**

ISBN 1-58660-999-8

COMPASSION'S CHARM

*Our mission is to publish and distribute inspirational products offering
exceptional value and biblical encouragement to the masses.*

PRINTED IN THE U.S.A.

one

January—Brenham, Texas

Rachel Morton had already waited thirty minutes to see the court-appointed attorney, and now she would have to wait another hour. Hunger clawed at her stomach. Thirst left her throat dry and scratchy, but if she left Adam Raeburn's office, she might ruin her chances to obtain custody of her three children.

"I don't want to cancel my appointment," Rachel said to Mr. Raeburn's secretary. "I can look at these magazines until he arrives."

The secretary swung her chair around to face Rachel. The tall, thin woman sighed. "Mrs. Morton, my name is Anna Carlson. I heard your stomach growling from over here. It's nearly lunchtime. Let me get you a sandwich and something to drink from the deli across the street."

Touched by the woman's offer, Rachel considered accepting. She'd skipped breakfast, or rather she didn't have anything in her efficiency apartment to eat. Last night she'd eaten a bowl of vegetable soup and a roll at the restaurant where she worked.

"Won't you let me order something for you?" Ms. Carlson asked. Sincerity emitted from her kind eyes while the scent of strawberry from a burning candle filled the spacious office.

Rachel's hunger was not the secretary's problem. "No thank you, Ma'am. I'll manage until after my appointment with Mr. Raeburn."

"Honey, you're going to wither up and blow away at this rate."

Rachel smiled. Not many folks cared about her these days,

and she appreciated every kind word and gesture from those who did. "I'll be fine."

Ms. Carlson clamped her hands on her knees as though undecided about whether to rise from the chair or stay seated. "Well, I'm ordering us both something, and I will be expecting you to eat."

"Oh, I can pay. I'm not really hungry."

"Fine. You can pay the next time." Anna Carlson swung back around to her desk and picked up the phone. She punched in a few numbers. "This is Anna. What's the special today?" She nodded. "Good, bring me two of those."

With a satisfied grin, Ms. Carlson replaced the phone on the cradle. "You will eat, Mrs. Morton. The special today is roast beef on marble rye with lettuce and tomato. Also you will have a side order of mustard potato salad, chips, a pickle, and raspberry iced tea—sweetened of course."

Rachel laughed. "Sounds good to me."

Ms. Carlson wiggled her shoulders and returned to the files on her desk. "Well, I'm not having any skinny girl pass out in my office."

Rachel moistened her lips. "Ms. Carlson, is Mr. Raeburn as friendly as you are?"

The woman glanced up and glowered. "The name is Anna. Now that we've established the formalities, I'll tell you the truth. I have a much nicer disposition, make better coffee, and treat the clients like royalty. Mr. Raeburn, on the other hand, is so dedicated to his work that he sometimes forgets his manners. You might say he's intense."

"I heard he was Christian."

Anna shook a finger at her. "I knew I'd seen you somewhere before. Must have been at church—Brenham's Community?"

"Yes, Ma'am. Pastor Johnston recommended this office."

"Ah, now I understand. Don't you worry a bit about Mr. Raeburn. He loves the Lord, and he'll do a fine job for you. He never does anything halfway."

What if you've spent time in prison? "I'm a little nervous."

"Of course you are. He'll be here before you know it. Just think, you'll have a full tummy when you meet with him, and he won't be serenaded by your rumbling insides."

Rachel eased back in the soft chair. If only her problems could be solved by eating lunch. She closed her eyes and tilted her head back to stretch achy neck muscles. So many mistakes. So many consequences. Would it ever end?

Anna knew why she was here, and she'd been kind enough not to say a word. *I see you lost your kids. Oh my, and you've spent six months in prison. Your husband was killed in a bad drug deal? And you think you can get your children back?*

Rachel pulled at her ear; it had once held seven earrings. At one time, body piercing had appealed to her. Her hair had been spiked orange and fuchsia, and she'd worn clothes so tight and short that it shocked her to remember them. Two years ago, all that changed. Twenty-eight years old, and she'd finally decided to grow up. Odd, when she made a rededication to the Lord, she thought life would be easier. Instead, the problems grew worse. God did help her through the trial, sentencing, and the six months in prison. He'd taken all those months to mold her into the beginnings of the woman He wanted her to be. God had a purpose for her life, and she intended to stick to Him like glue so He could work it out.

She simply hoped His plans included the return of her children. But the consequences of her past behavior might not warrant the joys of motherhood.

She glanced down at her skirt and gave it a tug, hoping the length was appropriate. She'd purchased it from Goodwill when she needed something to wear for job interviews. Mom had her clothes at the farm where the children lived, but Rachel hated to ask her parents if she could climb into the attic and retrieve them. At one time they would have done it. They would have done anything to help her rehabilitation. This time, however, Rachel needed to do all the work on her own.

The outside door to Adam Raeburn's office opened, and a young man entered carrying two small white bags. The smell of roast beef and delicious rye bread wafted across the room—a most pleasant aroma. Her stomach cried out.

"I heard that," Anna said. "Come on, Honey, and get yourself something to eat."

Shortly after they finished, Attorney Adam Raeburn entered his office. He hurried in, reminding Rachel of a linebacker, and stopped abruptly at Anna's desk.

"I'm sorry I'm late. When did Mrs. Morton reschedule?"

Anna pointed to Rachel. "She decided to wait."

Mr. Raeburn stiffened. "I'm already behind." He glanced back at Rachel and nodded. "I'll be right with you, but our meeting will be short."

Rachel instantly noted his stone-hard features: narrowed dark eyes, lips pressed together like he'd just sucked on a lemon, and a firm jaw. His navy suit fit her sinister impression of him, right down to his wingtipped shoes. She trembled. Mr. Raeburn wasn't what she'd prayed for or expected. She thought a Christian court-appointed attorney would smile at a prospective client and apologize for being late. At least, that's what Rachel wanted to believe.

She sat fifteen more minutes for a total of almost two hours. If he hadn't been recommended by Pastor Johnston, she'd have left a long time ago.

The phone rang, and Anna snatched it up. She nodded at Rachel and smiled. "Go on in, Honey. Mr. Raeburn can see you now."

Rachel's knees threatened to give way, and a sudden wave of chill bumps rose on her arms. She realized a prayer stood between her and his office, but for the life of her, she couldn't form the words. "Thank you," she said, "for lunch and being so kind."

"You're welcome. Now, don't you worry about a thing. Mr. Raeburn is the best."

Gripping the doorknob with a sweaty palm, Rachel twisted it as though something or someone formidable stood ready to pounce on the other side. She stepped through the threshold, and all thoughts of courage drained from her heart and mind. If not for a passionate longing for her children, she'd have fled from the office.

"Sit down, Mrs. Morton." Mr. Raeburn didn't even lift his gaze from the open file on his desk. "You've sat in my office all morning, and I apologize for the inconvenience."

"That's all right," she said. "I was told you are the best, and right now I need all the help I can get." Two wooden chairs were placed in front of his desk, and she elected to take the one closest to the door.

He focused his attention on her, and she quivered. "I don't bite, Mrs. Morton. At least not in the first ten minutes."

She supposed his faint grin was aimed at helping her relax, but it didn't happen. With folded hands anchored to her lap, she moistened her lips and waited. By now, she'd become an expert in that department.

"I see you want to file for custody of your three children." He continued to concentrate on the open file. "Autumn Winds Morton, age nine; Summer Angel Morton, age eight; and Rocky Waye Morton, age three." He peered at her over his reading glasses. "Names are a bit creative."

"Yes, Sir." Rachel willed her voice to stop shaking. It didn't work. She'd been criticized enough about her children's names. Frankly, she thought the choices were perfectly suited for them.

"Currently, your parents, Archie and Thelma Myers, have custody."

"Yes, Sir."

Mr. Raeburn sighed. "And you have once-a-week supervised visits with your parents present. How are those going?"

She shifted in the hard chair. "I haven't seen them for a few weeks, since Christmas."

His eyes narrowed, just as they'd done in the front office. "Why is that?"

"I work from the time they get up until after their bedtime."

"Seven days a week?"

Her heart refused to slow down. "I have Saturday mornings

free and Sundays until three o'clock. I'm a waitress at Brenham's Country Cooking."

"That doesn't tell me why you haven't seen them since the holidays."

Rachel took a deep breath. "Autumn, the oldest, feels uncomfortable around me. Summer cries when the visit is over, and Rocky acts like he doesn't know me. I couldn't afford the gifts they wanted, although my dad purchased something special for each one and put my name on the gift tag."

Mr. Raeburn's look pierced her very soul, as though he accused her of being unfit, and why not? "Then what is the reason for wanting custody?"

"I need to explain myself."

He leaned back in his chair: leather, plush, undoubtedly comfortable. "Yes, Mrs. Morton. Start from the beginning and tell me everything. I have notes here in my file, but I want to hear your story."

Rachel cleared her throat. "I don't have a good reputation here in town. I was a problem kid—always into trouble. I married a dealer right out of high school. I was pregnant and thought having his baby would solve all my problems. For seven years I used drugs and gave birth to Autumn, Summer, and Rocky. Luckily, none of the children appears to have been affected by my substance abuse." She took a deep breath.

"Right after Rocky was born, Slade and I were arrested for possession and a few other charges. My parents took the children while we were in jail so they wouldn't be put in foster care. I realized my life with Slade was going nowhere, so I left him and checked into drug rehab. Once I was released, I returned home in an effort to live clean and be a proper mother to my kids. During this time, Slade was shot and killed in a bad drug deal. I know my parents weren't excited about me coming back, but they gave me another chance." She paused and straightened in the chair.

"I started going to church and made a rededication to the Lord. I'd been brought up in church, and I had no excuse for the things I'd done—especially to my children. Then my past caught up with me again, and I had to go to trial for auto theft. I'd driven a car for Slade to make a drug deal, not knowing he'd stolen the vehicle. So I went to prison for six months. I was released eight months ago." Rachel leaned in closer to Mr. Raeburn. "I'm a Christian, and I know I'm forgiven. I also realize my worthless past. There's nothing to show for my life of any value except my kids. I want a chance, with God's help, to be a good mother."

There, she'd said it all, none of which he couldn't learn by searching records and talking to her parents and Pastor Johnston.

He nodded. His face still resembled stone. She wished he'd say something, anything. "Have you told me absolutely everything? Because you know I'll learn the truth eventually."

Tucking a stray hair behind her ear, Rachel braved forward. "Slade can't hurt me or frighten the children anymore. He had an ugly temper when he was drunk," she said. "I don't have a boyfriend. In fact, I keep to myself. My probation officer can vouch for me. I've done everything she has required or suggested."

Mr. Raeburn picked up a pen and jotted something on his notepad. "What does love for your children mean to you?"

Startled, she groped for words. "It means I'd do anything for their safety and well-being. Their needs come first. It means reading and applying books about child care and parenting. It means enrolling in classes to ensure I learn how to be a good mother. It's all about them, not me."

He nodded. "In the process of trying to secure legal custody of your children, I want you to remember what you've just told me."

"Yes, Sir."

"Back to my original question. I need clarification. You desire custody for children who are uncomfortable around you. Right?"

When he said it, her reasons sounded selfish, pathetic.

"Yes. I don't think they will feel that way once they are living with me."

"Do you feel your parents are doing a good job?"

"Definitely. Those kids are their whole world."

"Are they asking to retain custody?" he asked.

"I'm sure they will."

Mr. Raeburn said nothing for several moments. Rachel shivered in the cool office. Maybe this hadn't been such a good idea, but she felt God telling her the time had come to step up to her responsibilities. Besides, she loved her children. They were the joy of her life outside of her relationship with God.

"Let me give you an idea of what you're facing," he said.

She pulled a pad of paper and a pen from her purse, then lifted her gaze to meet his.

"First of all, there will be a hearing. At that time, both sides will express their reasons to a judge as to why the children should be in the custody of one home or the other. Both sides will have witnesses. A court-appointed child psychologist and Child Protective Services will be involved. The judge listens to the testimonies, reviews documents, and decides whether the case will be heard by him or will be a trial by jury."

The mention of standing before a judge caused her to tremble. "I didn't know how involved it would be," she said.

Mr. Raeburn paused while she continued to write. "If the case goes to trial, nothing will be hidden. All of your history will be brought to the jury's attention. The more money your parents are willing to spend, the more information will come to light. It is brutal."

Mr. Raeburn must have believed she had no case. He showed no emotion, only a cold, hard facade. She swallowed hard. "I understand, but I have to do this. What is the one thing I can do right now to help get my kids back?" she asked.

Mr. Raeburn offered a grim look. "Change your past." He hesitated before beginning again. "You have indicated a need for representation in this pursuit. Pastor Johnston indicated belief in your rehabilitation, which is why I took this case as a favor to him."

"I thought you were court-appointed."

"No, Mrs. Morton. Greg Johnston is a good friend." Before she could object to the arrangements, he added, "On the other hand, I'd like for you to examine your motives and your resources. After you leave this office, ask yourself: Why do I want my children? How can I take care of them? Where will we live? Am I the best person to do the job? When you can answer those questions, call me, and we'll set up another appointment."

"Is there anything else I can do?" she asked.

"Yes, there is." He closed the file before him and laid it on the corner of his desk. "Go see your children. A parent must take the good with the bad. If there are initial problems with the visits and you are avoiding the kids, do you think a judge will return them to you?"

He was right. She'd taken the coward's way out. "I understand, and I'll make the necessary arrangements."

"Good." He stood, indicating her dismissal.

"Thank you for taking time with me," she said. "I have prayed about this, and I believe children belong with a mother who cares."

He glanced away. "We'll talk in a few days."

Rachel exited his office and looked for Anna. She'd been a buffer in an attempt to soothe her ragged nerves, but the kindly woman wasn't at her desk. Maybe she'd overheard the conversation with Mr. Raeburn and slipped away. Maybe she'd formed an opinion about Rachel's ability to care and provide for her children. Maybe she believed, like so many others, that Rachel had destroyed her life and didn't need to ruin her children's lives.

She'd stammered and stuttered through her appointment with Mr. Raeburn. Rachel saw the look in his eyes. Trash. No skills. A police record. Why did she think she could be a fit mother?

two

From his office window, Adam Raeburn stood and watched Rachel Morton rush down the sidewalk. What was her hurry anyway? Then he saw her swipe at her eyes and realized he'd pushed her to tears.

I could have been gentler, but representing her in court to gain custody of those poor kids went against everything I believe. He had no idea why she thought any judge would let her have them. Adam released a breath and jammed his hands into his pockets. Glancing out the window again, he saw her pull away from the curb in a beat-up car that looked older than she.

Pathetic, very pathetic. Rachel Morton most likely knew more about selling drugs than mothering three children. He felt certain her kids were better off with the grandparents. She didn't look the part of an addict, but with so much of society plunging into the drug world, who knew the typical habits and descriptions? A pretty little thing. . .

The door opened, and Anna walked in. Adam took one look at her determined stance, and he knew he was in for a lecture on preconceived ideas.

"I passed Rachel on the way out of the building. She had huge tears streaming down her face."

"You comprehend client confidentiality. I can't tell you what we discussed."

"I understand perfectly. I simply hated to see her cry. Her parents are friends of mine, and I have a pretty good understanding of the situation."

Adam expelled a heavy sigh. "She told me the whole story, including how she has made a mess of her life."

"And she wants her kids back?"

"Anna. You already know that."

14

"What a mess. Archie and Thelma will be devastated. They love those children."

Adam picked up Rachel's file from his desk. "I don't think she has much of a chance, at least not without some work."

Anna crossed the distance to face him. "Are you willing to put some elbow grease into this case?"

"I don't want any part of it. You know how I feel about unfit parents. Since you know the grandparents, you must feel the same."

Anna shrugged. "I want whatever suits God. Don't you?"

A flash of irritation warmed him. "Are you trying to make me feel guilty, because if you—"

"I'm not doing anything of the sort. I will suggest you pray about this before you turn down her request." With those words, Anna turned and left the office. She closed the door just a bit harder than Adam would have preferred.

He despised charity cases, but Pastor Johnston had gotten him into this and now Adam had to follow through. Rachel had believed he was a court-appointed attorney, and she hadn't appreciated finding out otherwise. But desperation caused people to conduct themselves in strange ways. Her nervousness today convinced him that her brains must be mush after all the drugs. Those children's names were another source of his contention. Whatever happened to traditional and sensible selections?

Adam's conscience began to needle him. He certainly had left his Christlike attitude tucked in his Bible. The poor woman might very well be sincere, otherwise why would the pastor recommend he take her case as a favor?

His thoughts trailed back to his brother. His lazy, partying sibling never had money to feed and support his son, which left Adam caring for the boy most of the time. The whole thing with his brother and now Rachel left a bitter taste in his mouth. Dealing with substance abuse on the home front was bad enough, but now he had the same issues in his law practice. What would his other clients think?

Anna's words bannered across his mind. If he took on

Rachel's case, then he'd have to prove her rehabilitation to the court. He rubbed his face. Rachel might decide to drop the matter. After all, he did ask her to think about it for awhile. If she considered her definition of love, she'd see those kids were better off with the grandparents. Holding on to that noble theme, he closed Rachel's file and attempted to concentrate on something else.

His mind tormented him and refused to let him go. He picked up the phone and dialed Greg Johnston's number.

"Good afternoon, Greg. This is Adam. I don't want to take up much of your time, but I wanted to talk to you about Rachel Morton. She just left my office."

"I'm glad she kept her appointment. Frankly, she's so insecure, I wondered if she'd follow through."

Adam rubbed his temples. Why did he think he was about to regret ever considering taking on this case? "She gave me her background information, and I have no reason to believe she lied. For that matter, why would she want to create such a colorful past?" He paused. "I'm sorry, Greg. You don't need my sarcasm."

"That's all right. I'd rather you vent your frustrations at me than anyone else."

Adam chuckled. Greg always had a good spin on things. "Thanks. My problem is the situation looks dismal. I probably should have questioned her more about employment, job skills, and the like, but I didn't."

"I understand completely. On the surface, she doesn't have a lot going for her. I told her to be perfectly honest with you about her background. Let me fill you in on what she's done since she found the Lord."

Good, I need it. Adam pulled out a legal pad and grabbed a pen. "Okay, fire away."

"Before the trial that sent her to jail, she started helping at her mother's boutique shop. Did an excellent job. She was in church every time the door opened, got involved in a Sunday school class, spent quality time with her kids. In other words, she was well on her way to total rehabilitation. At that time, she lived with Archie and Thelma, and I counseled the whole family." Greg paused for a moment, as if he imagined Adam jotting down the words.

"Then after her sentencing, instead of growing bitter, she told me of her plans to talk about Jesus to the other women. The truth is she took the gospel to a bunch of hardened inmates. During this time, Archie and Thelma grew more attached to the kids, and, for the first time, those kids had true stability. I don't doubt Autumn, Summer, and Rocky love their mother; they simply are afraid to trust. The oldest one has chosen to separate herself from Rachel while the other two respond in tears and bad behavior."

"What a sad mess." Adam meant every word.

"There's more. Currently, she attends a different church service than her parents so the children will not be upset. The last time she visited them, the oldest told her she didn't want to see her again. Rachel has complied."

"Greg, giving up doesn't help her case."

"I understand, and I agree. As much as I am on her side, I see the children's turmoil. She is working double and triple shifts to pay bills and save money for when she has custody again. Today she took off a few hours to see you."

"And I kept her waiting for two hours." His insensitive attitude disgusted him.

Greg sighed. "She'd have waited two more at the thought of you possibly being able to help her."

"So she's living alone and working all kinds of hours to save money."

"And she's talking to someone at the community college about starting classes at the end of summer, and I'm counseling her on a weekly basis."

Suddenly, Adam wanted to crawl under his desk. He'd taken this woman, chewed her up, and spit her out into the gutter. What a great Christian example. The thought made him sick—of himself.

"I wish she'd shared those ideals with me," Adam said. "Of course, I didn't give her much of an opportunity."

"I know the case doesn't look good, but she's trying very hard. I will do whatever it takes to help her."

I should have told her the same thing. "Thanks, Greg. I'll look into the case a little further and keep you informed."

"Great. Oh, wait a minute. Rachel just walked into my office."

Adam cringed. "May I have a word with her please?" He heard Greg speak to the young woman.

"Hello." Her voice sounded full of emotion, sinking Adam even deeper into conviction and regret.

"Rachel, I appreciate your talking to me today. I apologize for being late and for my rudeness. I'm also sorry for not listening to your whole story."

Silence reigned for what seemed like several seconds. He imagined the slender young woman with her short, dark hair and enormous green eyes. She was probably fighting for control.

"That's all right, Mr. Raeburn. If I take the time to think about my past, I wonder why any judge would award me custody of the children. I want to think and pray about our discussion and call your office in a few days like you suggested. Is that appropriate?"

"Absolutely. Is the pastor still available?"

In the next instant, Greg was back on the phone. "Thanks, Greg. I'll see you later at the stress-management class." Adam chuckled. "Looks like I really need it."

❧

Rachel clocked in at Brenham's Country Cooking with five minutes to spare. Because the restaurant was located on Main Street in the historical district and within a few blocks of her second-floor apartment, she normally didn't have to race for time. But today she'd spent nearly an hour with Pastor Johnston, and the time had nearly slipped away. He listened to her concerns and her weeping about Adam Raeburn's hostility—and the reality of the truth. Then she'd asked the pastor for advice.

"Adam's a good attorney and a good man. I know he can

be blunt, but he'll be the first to admit he's wrong. Give him another chance."

Remembering another comment Mr. Raeburn had made, she said to the pastor, "I thought he was a court-appointed attorney, but he's not. He's representing me as a favor to you. For some reason, I thought when you recommended him that he took on cases like mine. How will I ever pay him?"

"Rachel, he doesn't expect payment. Adam and I are good friends—and he knows I wouldn't send him a case that I didn't believe in."

All the more reason why I should walk away from this.

"Promise me," Pastor Johnston began, "you will see this through. I know you want those children back, and Adam knows his stuff."

She agreed, but her heart threatened to betray her feelings. The old Rachel would have skipped work and gotten high. The thought sickened her, and she silently prayed for all those people who chose to ignore their problems and indulge in substance abuse.

Later on at the restaurant, the evening crowd filled both the front dining area and the back room designated for private engagements. She loved her job and she loved people. The combination made her work speed by, even if sore feet and a tired body often accompanied her home.

While standing beside the computer to punch in an order, she glanced about the popular restaurant. The outside and the inside followed a country theme of blue and white, accented with splashes of yellow. White rocking chairs lined a wraparound porch, and a collection of birdhouses rested beside the rockers and among twisted vines on the porch walls. In front of the restaurant on the right side of a stone walkway, a white picket fence surrounded a small garden filled with herbs and vegetables. On the left side, assorted annuals and perennials added splashes of red, blue, yellow, and orange. Inside the restaurant, blue gingham tablecloths and yellow daisies decorated round wooden tables, and the same decor covered the rectangular tables of the booths along the walls. More bird-houses and an assortment of miscellaneous antiques provided a cheery and warm atmosphere. An old wood-burning stove sat in the middle of the front dining area and held the owner's recipe books for the patrons to purchase.

Every night had a special, and tonight—Tuesday—was no exception. A huge blackboard read cheese-stuffed meatloaf, scalloped potatoes, green beans, white and bran yeast rolls, and fresh peach cobbler with vanilla bean ice cream. Rachel grinned. And that didn't include the regular menu. Sometimes she helped the owner with breakfast, a hearty meal served from six to ten. More times than she cared to remember, Rachel had worked from five in the morning until after ten o'clock at night. She didn't mind, except her feet and back screamed in protest. The more money she made, the more money went into her savings account at the local bank.

"Rachel, can you take a few extra tables tonight?" the owner, Joan Taylor, asked. "Looks like one of the girls isn't going to make it."

"Sure." Rachel glanced at her boss's round face and smiled.

"It's tables seventeen through twenty beside your section. You're a lifesaver. I've called Kelly to come in and give us a hand, but it will be at least forty minutes before she can get here. I'll be over to help as soon as I check on things in the kitchen."

"Got it," Rachel said. God was good, even if it meant a little more work.

Later at closing, she helped sweep and set up the tables for breakfast the following morning. Her tips had been good today. The extra tables had taken care of the shift she missed because of her appointment with Mr. Raeburn.

Lord, that man was nasty to me today—self-righteous too. I can tell You this because You already know my thoughts. If he is to help me get my kids back, I'll do whatever he says. But Lord, could You sweeten him up a little?

Mr. Raeburn had asked her a few questions about the children, questions she was to ask herself. *Why do I want my children? How can I take care of them? Where will we live? Am I the best person to do the job?* She needed to think about them and put together proper answers. She also told the attorney that she'd arrange a visit.

Rachel remembered her last visit with the children. She shook her head in an effort to push away the memories. As usual, Autumn refused to speak to her. No amount of prodding from her grandmother produced any communication until the little girl blurted out, "I hate you" and "Just leave us alone. We want to live with Grandma and Grandpa." Summer and Rocky had behaved badly, then Summer burst into tears when Rocky hit her. It was a nightmare, and Rachel vowed to not put them or her parents through another uncomfortable visit without a member of the Child Protective Services present to help keep peace. Rachel also saw the need for additional counseling and parenting classes for herself. She'd been reading books by Christian authors that Pastor Johnston recommended. All sounded wonderful to help her be the mother God wanted, if she could only find the time to absorb and practice the techniques.

"Rachel, I hate to ask you this." Tired lines etched Joan's forehead and deepened at the corners of her eyes. "I have a food order coming at six-thirty in the morning. Can you possibly come in around six and take care of things while I handle it?"

"I'll be here," she replied as cheerfully as possible. "I will need a few minutes sometime during the morning to call Mom, probably during a break."

"Sweetie, there is no need to even ask such a thing, and don't use your morning break. Make the call when we have a lull."

"Thanks, I need to make an appointment to see my kids."

Joan tilted her head and offered a sympathetic smile. "You arrange it, and we'll work it out here. Those babies are the most important things in your life."

Rachel nodded. "I keep remembering the last visit, but I'm prayed up and I've read another book since then. Poor little Autumn can't be blamed for her feelings. I know I'm an embarrassment to her, and I'm sure her little friends tease her about having a mother who's a jailbird." She removed a soiled, white apron from her yellow uniform and laid it over her arm. "But I love them, and I believe God will work it all out for the best."

Joan hugged Rachel's shoulders. "That's my girl. Keep the faith, I always say."

But what if my babies don't need me? What if Autumn's words were true?

For certain, she must convince Adam Raeburn that she had all the proper ingredients for being an excellent mother or the hearing would be a waste of his time—and her parents' money in contesting the case.

three

Adam lifted his computer case into the backseat of his car. Stealing a glimpse at his watch, he noted ten minutes until the first meeting of Greg's stress-management class.

"What I need is more hours in the day, more money, and a long vacation," he said to no one but a fifty-seven-variety dog who decided to use the rear left tire of Adam's car as a public rest room. "And fewer dogs."

The canine wagged his tail and headed toward Adam, but he ignored the animal and sunk into the driver's seat of his ultra-expensive sports car. A turn of the key and he was off to his class. Stress management had sounded like an answer to prayer when Greg first invited him to the class. At this very minute, Adam wondered how he'd fit it in every Tuesday night for the next six weeks. What was he thinking?

After the class, he'd scheduled a tutoring session with his nephew. The poor kid began junior high less than two months ago, and already progress reports indicated failing grades in English and math. The boy was smart, but he didn't have a reason to succeed. Once he finished with his nephew, Adam's computer case contained the files to two critical cases. Sleep had become a luxury.

His stomach growled and gurgled. All afternoon he'd meant to stop and eat, but the workload took precedence. Since the class started at six-thirty, Greg might have thought to provide a little food. Flipping up his console, Adam grabbed a peanut butter granola bar. In the next breath, he craved a bottle of water.

Without a doubt, Adam needed this class. If he didn't grasp a few tools to manage his fast-paced crazy life soon, he wouldn't have a life to manage. He parked his car and made his way inside the church to one of the adult Sunday school classrooms. An assortment of sandwiches, chips, and fruit with chilled bottles of water caught his attention. He stepped into the food line and tried not to look too ravenous.

Greg stood at the front of the room. "Thanks for attending this first session on stress management. I understand many of you came straight from work, so each week I'll have something here for you to eat. Feel free to refill your plates and drinks at any time. I wouldn't want any of you getting stressed out because you were hungry."

Laughter rose from the group. Adam took a generous bite of a smoked turkey sandwich. Things were looking better already. He studied his pastor and friend, a regular-looking guy—medium height, light brown hair, a wide smile, and a square jaw that gave him a bookish appeal.

"This is a six-week class in which we'll examine a biblical approach to handling stress. On your tables are outlines about what we'll cover. The homework is nothing more than reading Scripture passages."

Adam knew he could handle Bible reading. Greg's outline would force him to stay in the Word. He admitted his hectic pace often became the excuse for a shortened daily time with the Lord.

"Since this is our first night together, let's begin by each one of you introducing yourselves and stating why you have elected to take this class."

That will take until midnight—at least with mine.

Greg chuckled. "Keep your comments to three minutes, or we'll be here until midnight. But first I'd like to open our discussion with prayer."

More laughter echoed around the room, and Adam joined in. He'd committed to do something about the lack of control in his life, and this class seemed to fit the bill. He noted the different ages and backgrounds of the class members. Whether the circumstances mentioned were family-related problems, work, or a personal conflict, Adam identified with every man and woman as members stood, identified themselves, and briefly explained why they were there. He soon found himself praying for each person's recovery.

"Go ahead, Adam," Greg said.

Adam stood. "My name is Adam Raeburn. I'm an attorney here in Brenham. Aside from my busy practice, I'm supporting my brother and mentoring and tutoring his son. In addition, I'm restoring an old farmhouse, and I'm active in church service. In short, I'm overwhelmed and need direction."

The confession hadn't inflicted permanent damage. In fact, he felt better already.

After everyone had an opportunity to share, Greg pulled the discussion together. "In the time remaining, I'd like for us to discuss a verse listed on your outline. Matthew 6:27 asks, 'Who of you by worrying can add a single hour to his life?' " Greg rubbed the palms of his hands. "How many of you worried about getting to class tonight, wondered if you really had the time to commit, or wished you hadn't signed up at all?"

Slowly the hands rose until everyone in attendance laughed again.

"My point," Greg said. "I even had second thoughts about finding the time to facilitate this class!"

An hour later, Adam drove to his brother's apartment. Simply listening to other people's problems and discussing the sin of worry had helped him understand the value of placing every facet of his life with the Lord. He wondered if Rachel Morton had done the same thing.

❧

Rachel yawned and reached for a cup of coffee. Customers had kept her busy all morning, but what a good problem to have. Wednesday mornings always brought a group of teachers from the local elementary school and several gentlemen from a local retiree center. The combination kept her hopping, but she enjoyed every minute of it.

Finally she found a few moments to call her mother and set up a visit with her children. Joan had been so good to allow her the privacy of her office. What a dear, sweet lady. She'd given Rachel a job on her first day out of jail. Not many people displayed such trust. Joan stood as the epitome of Christian grace and love. She had no reason to care, except she walked in Jesus' footsteps and wanted to help others.

Rachel stared at the phone, and her stomach did a little flip. She shouldn't feel this apprehension. Mr. Raeburn had recommended it, and she did miss the kids. Before she went to jail, Rachel had the good fortune of living with them. Every day she saw their precious faces and took pride in making certain they were clean, fed, and loved. A tug on her heart nearly brought a flood of tears. She gripped the handle of the coffee cup, but the contents shook nevertheless. *Autumn, Summer, and Rocky.* How she craved the touch of their skin, the sight of milk mustaches, the scent of innocence, and the sound of giggles. Nothing could replace those cherished remembrances.

Rachel couldn't change what she'd done to lose them, but she could step forward and make every day count for something. With trembling fingers, she punched in her parents' number. Normally, her mother didn't work on Wednesday mornings. She answered on the fourth ring.

"Hi, Mom. Are you doing okay?"

Obviously startled, her mother hesitated. "Hi, Rachel. I'm doing just fine. Are you off today?"

"No, I'm calling from work. How are the kids?"

"Pretty good. Rocky has a cold. The girls are enjoying school."

"Mom, I really want to see them."

"Rachel, I know you do." Mom released a sigh. "I'm simply remembering the last time."

"That's why I haven't called or tried to visit. At first I thought a representative of Child Protective Services needed to present, but I've changed my mind. I simply need to try harder. Can we arrange something? I know your schedules are full and I work—"

"I can't stop your visits, Honey. I'm merely thinking about what is best for the kids."

A twist of anger warmed Rachel's face. "I want whatever is best for them too. You and Daddy are doing a wonderful job. I simply want to be their mother."

"You had your chance. They need an opportunity to grow up normal and happy. Your dad and I have provided that atmosphere."

Rachel blinked back the tears and took a drink of the hot coffee. "I understand, Mom, and I want those things for them too. For a long time, I believed it was best for them to be with you. Now, I think differently. I'm working on a—"

"Plan? I've heard your plans for years, and that's all they are."

"This time it's different." Rachel squeezed her eyes shut. "Mom, God is showing me things every day about myself—good and bad."

Silence fell between Rachel and her mother.

"All right. We could try lunch after church on Sunday."

Rachel swallowed the liquid emotion. "Thank you, thank you so much."

She replaced the phone and reached for a tissue. Taking a deep breath, she downed the rest of the coffee. Through the closed door, she could hear the sounds of an early lunch crowd making their way into the restaurant. This job helped her keep a finger on her sanity. Serving others, making sure their needs were met gave her purpose, even on days like today when she'd work until closing. This afternoon on her next break, she'd call Mr. Raeburn's office and schedule another appointment.

"Rachel?" Joan knocked at the door.

"Come on in."

"Hey, Honey, everything okay?" The kind, round face reminded Rachel of a character from an old movie—the one everyone wanted as their mother.

Rachel nodded. "I'm having lunch with my parents and the children on Sunday."

"Wonderful. These pesky problems will work out. You have a lot of great people praying for you."

"I need a mountain of prayers." She stood from the desk.

"Guess I'll head back to work."

"There's a gentleman here for lunch who has requested you."

Rachel grinned, assuming the man was an older gentleman who loved to tease. "I'm on my way."

Joan reached down to hug her. "You are such a blessing. I can't imagine running this place without you as my backup. No one else is willing to pitch in whether I ask or not. And, my dear girl, you have great business sense."

Mom had said the same thing when Rachel helped with her mother's boutique. The compliment lifted her spirits then and now.

Joan handed her a clean apron, and Rachel stepped out into familiar surroundings.

She glanced across the restaurant to her section of tables. There sat Adam Raeburn. She inwardly sighed and pasted a smile on her face. At least she wouldn't have to call him this afternoon. Another thought slammed her senses. Mr. Raeburn could have requested her so he could deny her request for legal assistance. She didn't remember ever seeing him there before, not that she paid much attention to all the customers—only the nice ones.

Shame on you, Rachel. He did *apologize.*

Mr. Raeburn looked up from the menu and grinned like they were old friends. The gesture looked sincere, and she moved toward his table.

"Hello, Mr. Raeburn. Did you ask for me?"

"I did. I wanted to see where my newest client worked."

She massaged her cold arms. "You mean it?"

"Absolutely, unless you've found another attorney with better manners."

"No. . .no, I haven't." She stopped in midsentence. "I'm sorry. That sounded rather bad, didn't it?"

He chuckled. When he did, Rachel saw a new side of him, rather likable. "When do you have time for an appointment? I'll do my best to stay on time."

"I have tomorrow morning free until ten-thirty."

"How about nine o'clock?"

She relaxed slightly. "Perfect. Now, what can I get you to drink?"

"Sweet tea, please. And I already know I want the honey-mustard grilled chicken sandwich and a garden salad with ranch dressing on the side." He nodded and handed her the menu. "I never can resist Joan's key lime pie, so I might as well order it too."

He must have been to the restaurant before. Odd, she'd never noticed him. A man as good looking as he would have been hard to miss. During the meal, Mr. Raeburn maintained a pleasant demeanor, even generously tipping her when he left. Something must have changed his attitude, evidence of God working overtime.

Rachel could barely contain her excitement the rest of the day. Her aching feet and back seemed only a minor annoyance with the good news from Mom and Mr. Raeburn. After closing, she rewrote the answers to his questions. The process of putting her thoughts into words always frustrated her. As soon as she finished, another word sounded better than something she'd written. She couldn't blame her past substance abuse; she'd always had problems focusing when under pressure. Finally, when the hour reached nearly one in the morning, she made a few notes about her plan and hoped Mr. Raeburn didn't ask for the jumbled mess.

Rachel refused to think of the consequences of making another bad impression.

four

Adam shifted the papers on his desk, knocked his coffee cup, and grabbed it just before it soaked the legal documents before him. He was off to a great start. *Stress free. Stress free.* If he repeated those two words enough, he'd believe them.

His cell phone rang, interrupting his determination to not let circumstances control him. A glance at the caller ID caused him to cringe. His brother never phoned on Adam's cell unless an emergency slapped him in the face, like being in jail.

"Hey, Rob. What's happening?"

"I'm not in jail if that's what you're thinking."

"Good news."

"Leave the sarcasm for the courtroom, Adam. I've got a problem with Bud. He got himself in trouble at school. Looks like the rug rat went to school drunk and got expelled. What can you do to get him back where he belongs?"

Adam pictured his 350-pound brother sprawled out on a worn sofa, taking blood pressure medicine with a beer. "He's twelve years old. Where did he get the stuff?"

Rob swore, and Adam held the phone away from his ear. "How would I know?" Rob asked. "I can't keep track of him every minute of the day. Right now, he needs to be in school and not bugging me."

Adam realized the futility of lecturing his brother, and right now he needed details. "What exactly did the school say?"

"Three days' suspension and mandatory counseling."

Adam heard a click that sounded like a can of beer being opened. "What was that?"

"What's it to you? I need something to calm my nerves."

"Getting drunk before nine A.M. makes perfect sense."

"I've got to keep up with my kid."

Listening to his brother criticize his son infuriated Adam. "Does Millie know? Or am I the first person you called?" Adam asked.

"You're the lucky first. Besides I don't know where she lives or works."

Adam expelled a breath. "Look, I have an appointment in five minutes. I'll call the school afterwards, then stop over to see Bud during the noon hour."

"Well, he ain't here." Rob belched, and Adam felt like throwing the phone.

"Find him and get him to the apartment." Adam made an effort to count to ten before he exploded. This new twist would make great material for next week's stress management class. Two minutes to nine and already out-of-control flares singed his heels.

The desk phone rang, and Anna announced Rachel had arrived. Adam took a deep breath. "Please, send her in. By any chance do you have time to get me a bagel and orange juice at the deli?"

"That bad?" He envisioned her eyes widening, indicating she already knew the answer.

"Not yet, but well on my way."

This time Rachel didn't look so much like a frightened mouse. She wore the gray skirt and white blouse from her previous appointment, and a worn straw purse draped from her shoulder. Poor thing probably didn't have much else. She greeted him politely, and he invited her to sit down.

"I have the answers to your questions, Mr. Raeburn." Her voice quivered while she pulled a small notepad from her purse.

"Excellent. Since you have them, I'll listen carefully to every word."

She smiled—a little shakily. "My motives for wanting custody of my children are simple. I love them, and I feel I am the best person to raise them. My past does nothing to help my cause, but the present and the future are what really count. Without the change God has made in my life, I'd gladly concede their care to my parents. I am saving every penny I can for emergencies once I have them again. Currently, I pay child support through the county for their care." She took a breath.

"Take your time. I don't have any pressing engagements." Actually he did, but she didn't need to know about his problems.

"I have more. Social Security is sending benefits from their deceased father to my parents, which will help me too when they are in my custody. I have looked at government housing, and I qualify for a three-bedroom apartment. I also qualify for government-subsidized daycare for Rocky and before-and-after-school care for the girls. As far as the future, in September I plan to start taking courses at Blinn College, and financial aid is available. I've already completed applications for grants. And I have made arrangements for a visit this Sunday."

Adam leaned back in his chair. "I'm impressed. You've done your homework."

Her slender shoulders lifted. "Thank you."

"Do you have this all written out?"

Rachel's face reddened. She stared at her hands folded in her lap, then lifted her gaze. "Mr. Raeburn, I've tried to write this out for you, but what is registering in my brain becomes a jumbled mess on paper."

"I tend to be the same way. Stress will do that to you."

She paused, as though searching for words.

For the first time Adam saw the loveliness of her smooth, creamy skin and the modestly applied makeup. Her delicate features and high cheekbones would rival those of any beauty queen.

She took a deep breath. "I've been told I have good business sense and management skills, but my best ideas are always in my head and not—"

She stopped midsentence, and Adam felt her pain of embarrassment.

"Rachel, a lot of people have this type of difficulty. When

I'm stressed, nothing makes sense."

"Really?" She brightened. "I've considered the possibility of a learning disability. That sounds a whole lot better than being stupid." She placed the notepad back into her purse. "Remember what you told me about a jury trial bringing up everything?"

Adam nodded.

"Would that include information like not being able to take tests in school? I keep praying about doing well in starting college classes, but I'm a little concerned." She shook her head. "I'm rambling. What I'm wondering is if my parents might use my problem against me."

Adam studied the young woman before him. She was definitely not stupid. "Are you telling me you have a potential learning disability or you simply have trouble responding correctly under pressure?"

"I think the latter. In school, I'd know the material, then freeze at test time."

"Neither one would be admissible in court unless you had difficultly holding down a job or had demonstrated an inability to manage your affairs." He picked up his pen and tapped it lightly on the legal pad before him.

"Mr. Raeburn, what are you thinking?"

He smiled. "I'm thinking that if you had been properly diagnosed as a child and learned more confidence in your accomplishments, maybe your path would have been different."

She nodded. "I can't really blame anything or anyone for my poor choices, but I do realize the struggles in school caused me to give up on myself. I've trained myself to learn by repetition. Anyway, my middle child, Summer, is struggling in school, and I fear she has inherited the same disorder."

"Possibly. And at this point, it probably wouldn't do any good to mention your concern to your parents." He made a few additional notes. "Other than taking tests, do you have any problems keeping a checkbook or getting to work on time?"

"No, Sir, absolutely not." She peered into his face for a

moment. "Do all lawyers go to this much trouble for their clients?"

He glanced up and smiled into her serious face. "Doesn't matter, because I do. I plan to talk to your probation officer and Joan. Are there any problems there? I imagine Pastor Johnston would give you a good recommendation."

"I'd prefer the pastor giving you a written one instead of calling him as a witness." She sighed. "He's close to my parents, and that might be uncomfortable. I wouldn't want to force him into taking sides. He's under enough pressure."

Considerate, determined to beat the odds against her. Get a grip, Adam. This is a client. "I understand. I'll see what Greg prefers. I need to look at all angles here, so I'm going to ask a few more questions. I'd like for you to give me your entire life story on tape. I don't expect you to do it in one setting, but it's important for me to know the truth about everything." She agreed, and he continued. "Do you have any outside interests, hobbies?"

Rachel's gaze swept to the window behind him. A faint smile tugged at her lips. "Maybe one."

"Do you mind sharing it with me? Sometimes hobbies and dreams pave the way for a future."

"I don't know." She shifted in the chair. "All right, Mr. Raeburn. I compose songs in my head. I hear the music and make up the words."

Startled, Adam wondered if she could possibly have real talent. Certainly this was worth investigating. "Do you play guitar or piano?"

"Piano. I took lessons for several years. God has given me the ability to hear songs and be able to sit down and play them."

"Have you done anything with this talent?"

She shook her head. "I'm much too shy, and I do have a problem reading music. My teacher used to play a song for me, and I simply copied her." Rachel laughed. "My method drove her crazy, especially when she wanted to teach theory. Besides, what good would this do to impress a judge?"

Adam made another note on his pad. "Most likely nothing."

"Autumn used to be interested in piano. She's the only one of the three who has expressed a desire to study music." Rachel hesitated. "Of course now she doesn't want to be around her mother. I'm sorry. That sounded like a poor-me attitude."

"No, it sounded honest. Starting this Sunday, you're going to be working on correcting the relationship with your children." He glanced at the clock on his desk. "We've accomplished quite a bit of work today. Let's meet next week after your visit and after I've had time to research a few things. If Thursday is good, check with Anna and schedule the same time."

"Thank you, Mr. Raeburn. I appreciate all you're doing for me."

"We're in this together. I'd like to pray before you leave."

"I'd be honored."

He bowed his head. "Heavenly Father, we ask for direction and guidance in this custody hearing. Give me wisdom and a listening ear for the matters that are important to You. Give Rachel peace and comfort in the tough days ahead. In Jesus' name, amen."

A nagging thought—the truth—moved him to speak. "I believe we have the beginnings for a good case, but we need to be prepared for the judge to rule against us. Are you ready to accept God's will through the judge in obtaining custody of your children?"

Huge tears rolled over Rachel's cheeks. "I want what's best for them, no matter what the outcome."

&

Rachel picked up her steps and hurried down the sidewalk to her car before the gray, swirling clouds opened up and drenched her. The law office was on West Alamo, not far from Blinn College and about ten minutes from her apartment. In thirty minutes her lunch shift began, and she always liked to be early.

Her mind drifted back to the meeting with Mr. Raeburn. He still frightened her a bit—or maybe it was his title and dark suit. She'd faced enough attorneys because of her illicit behavior to feel apprehensive in their presence. The ones who had represented her often acted as though she'd fried her brains, and the ones who prosecuted her didn't mince any words when it came to condemning her. Of course, how could she blame them? Fortunately, Mr. Raeburn didn't fall under either of those categories. Today had gone so much better than before. He treated her with respect and concern, a big switch from the previous appointment.

She appreciated his honesty and his Christian viewpoint. He didn't make promises he couldn't keep, and he made it evident that God might not choose for the children to live with her. The realization hit hard, and she refused to dwell on it. Rachel sensed God had a big lesson to teach her, and she hoped it began with faith and ended in the judge awarding her custody.

For certain, Pastor Johnston had led her to a wise attorney. She planned to follow Mr. Raeburn's suggestions and not let a poor visit with the kids on Sunday discourage her. The rest was up to God.

If Rachel dwelled on thoughts about the man for any length, she'd be tempted to think about him in another light. *What a cliché,* she thought. *The client feels a spark of romance for her attorney.* He'd displayed kindness and concern today, and his smile would melt an iceberg. Her thoughts reeled like an old movie. Caution took control, and she decided not to revisit those aspects of Mr. Raeburn again.

All of a sudden, raindrops pelted her body and splattered on the sidewalk. Thunder cracked and a bolt of lightning danced a jagged pattern across a blue-gray sky. The battering rain reminded her of life. Just when she believed the sun was shining, a storm shook her world.

five

The windshield wipers clicked back and forth in time to the contemporary Christian music on the radio. Adam glanced at an elderly couple huddled beneath an umbrella, taking a morning walk. Their stride seemed to be in rhythm to the music. He chuckled, but at the next stop sign, he allowed the words of the song to flow through him and penetrate his heart and mind. Sometimes the best form of worship came in a repeated phrase. *Lord, I want to be like You.*

Simple words with a depth of feeling. Following Jesus like a child appeared effortless until the believer met a brick wall. Sometimes the only way to get around life's obstacles was to chip a way straight through, and that's how Adam felt about the situation with his brother and nephew. Steadily, the bricks of sin and despair widened the gap between Rob and Bud. Rob lived from one sort of numbing to the other, and as much as Bud voiced hatred for his father, he headed in the same direction. No point in contacting the boy's mother. She didn't care about either of them.

Usually Adam could talk to Bud and help him make sense of the difficulties plaguing his young life, sometimes even see things from a biblical perspective. Although Adam took him to church and Sunday school every week, the boy had developed a nasty attitude toward anyone in a leadership position—including God. The truth of that was revealed in today's events. Adam wanted to turn Bud across his knee. He took a deep breath. Bud Raeburn, Adam's namesake, had stolen his heart a long time ago. But if the boy had gone to school drunk, he'd gone past the stage of warming his posterior for inappropriate behavior. Some type of discipline needed to be enforced, but what? Rob couldn't discipline himself, never mind his son, which meant Uncle Adam had his hands full—again. He remembered Greg stating Rachel had read parenting books. Adam needed to find out the names of those titles.

Adam had no intentions of going to the school and pulling a few strings. Bud had broken the rules, and now he must face the consequences. If Bud skated through this, the next incident would be worse.

Opening his car door, Adam peered up at the shabby, paint-chipped, two-story building that housed Rob and Bud's apartment. The front door hung on one hinge, and glass sprinkled the weed-infested front yard. His gaze trailed up to a broken window from Rob's apartment. He'd seen the filth and roaches inside. A few times, he'd hired a cleaning lady, but within a week the condition reverted to the usual chaos. Twice before, social services had pulled Bud from the home and allowed Adam to keep him. Back then, Rob wanted the boy and took steps to clean up his act and secure custody. Adam hoped this time his brother would give up the boy, and although the job looked formidable at best, Adam would gladly take him.

The steps leading upstairs creaked and groaned. He wondered how Rob's 350-pound frame kept from crashing through. At the top of the stairs, Adam didn't need to knock; the door stood wide open, and the stench of beer, vomit, and spoiled food attacked his senses.

Our mother would climb out of her grave if she knew how her oldest son lived.

Child Protective Services would love this. He compared Rob's situation with Rachel's. No matter how many times Bud had been yanked out of this dirt-infested hole, Rob always managed to get the boy back—and not always through Adam's help either. Rachel only wanted a chance to prove her mothering skills and a way to provide for her children. Right then, Adam renewed his commitment to help her. He might know very little about the woman, but what he did know impressed him.

"Come on in." Rob moved toward him, leaning from one foot to the other like a gorilla. "The kid ain't come back." He ran his fingers through greasy hair. "I've got his stuff in a box on his bed. Even if you got him back in school, I can't handle him anymore. Too much work."

Adam clenched his fists. "If I take him this time, you'll have to fight for custody."

Rob held up his hands in defense. His shirt gaped open, exposing a bare, hairy stomach. Adam strode past him, picked up the box, and left.

He tossed the box into his trunk. Pulling his cell phone from his pocket, he checked in with Anna.

"I'll be there later; I need to find my nephew."

"Runaway?"

"Sort of. He was expelled from school for drunkenness, and now I have to find him."

Oh Lord, what are You trying to teach me about children and their care?

Almost two hours later, Adam found Bud at a hamburger stand, drinking a cola. He didn't know whether to hug him or shake him until all the alcohol in his system spewed. All he could think of was mercy and grace—and right now Bud needed a whole lot of both. So did Adam.

"Hey." Adam sat across from him in a booth.

Bud's once walnut-colored hair now spiked orange and turquoise. It looked like he'd plucked peacock feathers and glued them on his head. He peered up, his blue eyes red and puffy. Judging from his wrinkled forehead, the boy must have a giant-size headache. "Did the cops send you?"

"No. I'm a free agent."

"This isn't funny, Uncle Adam."

"You're right." Adam stared into Bud's face and captured his attention. "You're in serious trouble."

The boy slid his paper cup away from him. "I don't know what the big deal is. I just wanted the day to go easier."

Adam lifted a brow. "Breaking rules only makes things harder." Bud started to speak but Adam raised his hand. "Right now you're going with me."

"Back home?"

"No. I have your things in the trunk."

"Child services again?"

Adam eyed him critically. Besides being expelled, Bud was about to learn how his father dealt with the problem. "Your dad thinks living with me is best."

Bud swallowed hard. "At least I'll get fed and live in a clean place."

"I'm not so bad?" Adam lifted a thumb under Bud's chin.

"Depends on how you feel about rules, studying, and church."

"We'll talk later, but right now I'm saying all three take top priority. You're going back to the office with me."

Bud stared emotionlessly, then scooted out of the booth. Adam didn't want to consider how the boy would spend the afternoon. He'd probably want to sleep, except Adam had another idea. First they'd stop at the library and pick up a book on alcohol abuse. A nice long book report was in order.

❧

If Rachel had thought the rain might deter customers, she'd made a grave mistake. The downpour brought not only a break in the sweltering heat but also folks carrying umbrellas into the restaurant for dinner. Every time she predicted the crowd size, another factor came into play; tonight was all-you-could-eat chicken-fried steak, mashed potatoes, dilled green beans, cornbread, and blueberry pie. Patrons managing everything from highchairs to false teeth devoured Joan's special.

Along about seven o'clock, Mr. Raeburn and a boy walked in—not exactly the type of clean-cut kid she'd expect from her attorney. She watched as the hostess ushered them to one of her tables. A few moments later, Rachel handed them menus. She noted the sullen look on the boy's face and his bloodshot eyes. Obviously, he didn't want to be there.

"I bet you're tired of seeing me," Mr. Raeburn said. He did have the prettiest white teeth and eyes that she originally assessed as dark were a deep blue.

"Absolutely not," she said. "And who is this handsome guy?"

"My nephew Bud." The boy did everything but sneer.

Rachel took their drink orders, and for the first time she felt a little sorry for her attorney. Adam's nephew looked like trouble with a capital T. He also looked and smelled like he needed a shower and clean clothes.

"Good to meet you, Bud." Not even a lifted eyebrow. She smiled anyway and took their orders. When she leaned to take Bud's menu, she smelled alcohol. The kid didn't look but a few years older than Autumn. Startled, she wondered how her precious daughter would hold up under peer pressure.

Later when the two were ready to leave, Mr. Raeburn pulled her aside and apologized for his nephew's rudeness.

"He must be having a bad day," she said.

"He's had a bad life. I know you smelled the alcohol on him." Mr. Raeburn shook his head and glanced at Bud standing at the front door. "I have a big job ahead of me."

"How's that?" Rachel's gaze trailed toward the boy.

"His mother deserted him. His dad, my brother, is a drunk, and he handed Bud over to me today."

Rachel realized a side of her attorney that was not only compassionate but overworked. "Sounds like both of you need prayers."

"Thanks, and yes, we need a dump truck full."

An uncomfortable moment followed before he smiled and left. Rachel didn't know what to say. She shrugged. Mr. Raeburn captured her curiosity tonight. Family law could encompass a whole lot of issues. Yet she wondered if the good-looking attorney often rescued those who dabbled in substance abuse.

❧

Before Rachel had time to fully prepare herself, Sunday morning arrived. She planned to attend the second worship service, the same as her parents and children. Mom hadn't invited her to sit with them, so she lingered in the parking lot until the last moment. The thought of hiding from her own children made her feel dirty. Then she remembered Autumn's words and realized the shame her children bore because of their mother.

Rachel couldn't change her past, and the day her children would feel any pride toward their mother remained in the future.

Walking down the hallway to the worship center, Rachel longed to stop into the nursery and see Rocky. They had a preschool church for little ones his age. If she did visit and upset him, the workers would inform Mom and Dad. Rachel picked up her pace past the nursery while her heart cried out to see her baby. She slipped into the back of the church and attempted to read the bulletin. Distracted with thoughts of lunch, she played and replayed conversation scenarios in her mind. Her attention swept to the middle front pew where her parents normally sat. There they were: Autumn and Summer, their long, dark, silky hair glistening in the light streaming through the stained-glass windows. *My green-eyed angels.*

Rachel felt the pew shift. On the other end, Mr. Raeburn sat with Bud. The boy looked even less excited than the other evening at the restaurant. On the other hand, Mr. Raeburn beamed. He wore a brown sports jacket over a cream shirt. She tugged at the skirt that he'd seen her wear twice before in his office. When he nodded at her, her stomach turned flip-flops.

She must push those romantic notions about Mr. Raeburn from her mind. He didn't need a high-maintenance woman who had enough problems to fill a legal journal.

The choir finished its special music, and she desperately tried to focus her heart and mind on the sermon. By the time Pastor Johnston finished, she fretted if seeing the kids were a good idea. When the last "amen" had been spoken at the close of the service, Mr. Raeburn handed her a note.

I'm praying for you! Let me know about the visit.

She glanced up from the note, and he grinned. What a good, kind man.

While waiting in the foyer for the first glimpse of her girls, several people greeted her—most of whom were customers. Autumn and Summer stood before her with Dad. He offered an encouraging smile and shifted his lean, lanky frame. Autumn wore an emerald green flowered skirt with a green knit top—and a frown. Summer wore a deep pink dress with a matching ribbon in her hair—and a shaky smile.

"Hi, Dad. Hi, girls." She hoped her voice sounded stronger than what she heard.

Dad wrapped his arm around her waist and kissed Rachel's cheek. "Your mom went after Rocky. She'll be here in a minute. What do you say to your mother, girls?"

"Hi, Mom," Summer said. "I'm glad you're having lunch with us."

Rachel bent and touched the little girl's soft cheek. "I'm glad too. You certainly look pretty this morning, and your grandma has fixed your hair so pretty." She wanted to hold Summer close, but in the past, those embraces ushered both of them into an emotional mess. Summer reached up and hugged her. The little girl shook in Rachel's arms, and when the two finally pulled away, Summer's eyes were watery.

Rachel peered into Autumn's face. She'd moved around to Dad and clung to his hand, her gaze fixed toward the front door. With an inward sigh, Rachel kneeled to Autumn. "How are you? How's school?"

"Fine." Autumn refused to look at Rachel.

With trembling hands, she reached up to touch her oldest child's face, but the girl stepped back.

"Don't touch me, please."

Rachel expected the animosity, but it still hurt. Mom showed up a moment later leading Rocky by the hand. He might be three years old and twice the size of the girls at his age, but he wasn't too much of a burden for Rachel. She swept him up into her arms and snuggled against his neck.

"Got you, Rocky." She planted a kiss on his nose.

"Really, Rachel. He's much too big for you to pick up. Why, you could hurt your back," her mother said.

"He's not so heavy." Rachel tickled him. "Although, I think he's almost big enough to carry me."

"I can." The little boy displayed his muscles and pressed his lips together. "See, I'm strong."

"That you are." Regret pierced her heart for all the time she was missing—important days and nights when her children grew and changed.

Mom had chosen a popular restaurant that catered to kids as well as adults. Rachel couldn't concentrate on the menu and asked Dad to order for her. Summer and Rocky chatted on both sides of her. They touched her and leaned on her despite Mom's chidings to sit up straight, don't lean on your mother, you don't have to touch her all the time. Autumn sat between her grandparents and remained aloof.

"How's school?" Rachel asked her oldest daughter.

"I told you before, fine." Autumn forked a French fry and dragged it across the ketchup on her plate.

"She's reading at seventh-grade level," Mom said. "Always has her nose stuck in a book."

"What kind of books do you like?" Rachel asked. *Please talk to me, Sweetheart.*

Autumn shrugged and popped the French fry into her mouth.

"Horses," Mom replied. "Those are her favorite."

"Wonderful," Rachel said. "What else are you enjoying in school?"

Autumn said nothing. Rachel's heart sank, and she blinked several times.

"She's started piano." Dad wrapped his arm around Autumn's shoulders. "Just like you, loves music." He grinned—that silly wide grin that made him look like a ten-year-old boy. He bent closer to Autumn. "Your mama has a real gift. She can listen to a song once and play it."

"Really?" Autumn's green eyes grew big. "I thought she took piano lessons. I can't do that."

"Well, it made learning theory very difficult," Rachel said. "I'm so proud you are taking lessons."

"Mama, would you play piano for us again?" Summer asked. "I loved hearing you sing too."

"Of course I will, that is if Autumn will play for us too."

Autumn shook her head. "I don't want to. Mom doesn't really care anyway."

six

On Monday, Rachel phoned Mr. Raeburn's office to confirm her Thursday morning appointment. The visit had been a strain on everyone involved, and Mom cut lunch short because of a migraine. Rachel understood her mother's method of handling uncomfortable situations.

On the morning of the appointment, Rachel wore her yellow uniform in case the appointment ran longer than anticipated. At least he wouldn't see her in that drab skirt again.

"What happened on Sunday?" Mr. Raeburn asked.

"Fairly smooth. Summer and Rocky were eager to see me and very affectionate, but Autumn obviously didn't want to be there." Rachel went on to relate in detail her mother's criticism of her in front of the children. "I need to ask her to not make critical remarks about me in front of them—even if they are true."

"I agree. Did your dad agree with her?"

"He seldom says anything, unless she's unusually harsh, but I know he does later because he's told me. The trouble is I thought Mom and I had worked through the differences between us before I went to prison."

"You might need to initiate a long discussion with her. Did you reschedule?"

"Yes, Sir. Dad suggested we try next Sunday again after church."

He picked up his pen and drummed it lightly on his desk. She'd been in enough appointments with him to understand the steady clicking coincided with his thinking. "Your dad is your cheerleader, isn't he?"

She nodded. "Always has been."

"And I imagine that causes conflict between them."

"Definitely, although Mom has calmed down considerably since her heart attack a few years ago."

Mr. Raeburn turned his head slightly. "Your mother has a heart condition?"

"Yes. A few years ago, she nearly died. Now, she takes medication and has cut back on her working hours." She startled. "She had a lot of migraines then too. I wonder if her heart is giving her problems."

He jotted down the information. "We might need to request a doctor's examination."

"Mr. Raeburn." When he glanced up, she continued. "Do you have any idea when we'll have a hearing?"

"I found out yesterday that we have a court date in two months, March nineteenth. And I think it's about time you started calling me Adam. Okay?"

"Sure." Moving to a first-name basis bothered her just a little. Those little romantic notions kept popping up, and as long as she referred to him as *Mister*, then any preconceived notions about him flittered away. This would make it a little more difficult.

"I talked to your guidance counselor at the college. She tells me you need to take a placement test. Do you have anyone helping you prepare for this?"

"Not exactly. The thought of doing poorly overwhelms me. Pastor Johnston is looking for a tutor, but nothing yet."

"It's important for you to take the test and show your seriousness about the future."

"I understand." Rachel felt the familiar sinking feeling. A nagging voice told her she was a loser, and she tried to shove it from her mind. "I need to be prepared. Tutors cost money, and I hate spending any on myself."

"If comprehension is the worst problem, perhaps I can help."

"How? Are you going to take the test for me?"

Adam chuckled, but she failed to find the predicament amusing. "Let me tutor you. Maybe your fear of tests isn't as bad as you think."

"That's great, even wonderful. One question though. When are you going to find the time to help me? Aren't you on overload already?"

"I can manage."

His reply didn't convince her. "I understand Pastor Johnston is giving a stress-management class."

"I'm taking it." He grinned.

"And aren't you now legal guardian of your nephew?"

"Right. Today is his first day back to school after suspension. He went to school drunk, and now he's paying the price." He raised a brow. "Twelve years old."

Rachel cringed. "That sounds like some of the stuff I used to do. More of a reason for me to not accept your offer."

"I have an idea."

"What's that?"

"Would you be willing to talk to Bud? Clue him in on what's ahead if he doesn't stop this pattern?"

She didn't have to think too hard. "Of course. I don't want to see anyone heading in that direction."

"Then let's swap—you counsel Bud, and I'll try to help you get over your fear of tests."

How could he be so confident? "I don't know about this." She rubbed her temples. "How would we work things?"

"I'll simply ask you to come for tutoring, and while you're there, you can ease into the things he needs to know."

"I know I've asked you this before, but do you always go to such lengths for your clients?"

He grinned. "Without a doubt."

Later when business slowed at the restaurant, she contemplated their deal. Her pride seemed to take over every rational thought, but reality finally ruled. Granted, she was a charity case, and Adam had initiated yet one more way to help her. But now a rebellious boy stood on the pivotal edge of making more bad decisions, and she had an opportunity to help him change. She'd been able to talk to a few female inmates while in prison. They said she had a knack for showing them God's love and making them understand their current path led nowhere.

Rachel desired to be used for God's purpose. Maybe talking to Bud fell under that category. She hoped so, for they had arranged to meet at Adam's home on Saturday evening. She'd been able to trade her dinner shift for a breakfast one.

Another thought occurred to her. Adam would not have any doubts about her stupidity after a few minutes quizzing her about simple material.

ಶಿ

Adam stood from his desk and watched Rachel walk away from the office building. Studying her when she left from an appointment had become a habit. What would he tell her if she happened to look up and see him gawking like a schoolboy?

And that's exactly how he felt. What he'd begun to feel for this lovely young woman went far beyond professional protocol. His feelings made no sense, and he'd asked God to show him why. Adam adored her smile, the way she reasoned, the way others came before her. It all led to a tremendous amount of respect for her. Poor woman, she'd be humiliated if she knew his romantic deliberations. Maybe he'd stop by for coffee tomorrow morning after dropping Bud off at school. If Rachel saw him more, she wouldn't be so flustered.

Instantly, he regretted his offer to help her prepare for the college entrance exam. Not only did he not have the time, but he also had his hands full with parenting Bud. Since his last stress-management class, he'd managed to take on two more projects—Bud and Rachel.

Lord, You know my schedule, my workload, and my many obligations. Let Your work prevail, and allow me to accomplish those things that matter to You.

Adam's thoughts turned to Rachel's children. He saw the older two last Sunday in church. Beautiful little girls. Looked like their mother. The same dark hair, pert nose, and perfectly oval faces. He wondered if they were as sweet.

Rachel had her hands full with those two and their brother,

but she appeared to grasp the enormity of the job before her. She understood responsibility and providing for her little family. Over two years ago, she'd made a conscious decision to build her life around Jesus and be a good mother. Unfortunately, her oldest daughter had chose, to reject her. Autumn could be hurt and fearful of her mother abandoning her again, so to protect herself, she erected a wall around her heart. Whatever the reason for Autumn's treatment of her mother, the change would take patience and love.

At six-forty-five the next morning, Adam joined the busy crowd inside the country restaurant for coffee. Seeing Rachel fresh and lovely prompted stirrings he thought he could dismiss. But it didn't happen. He chose to read over his notes for the morning's case and drink three cups of delicious, nutty-flavored coffee so he could savor the faint scent of raspberry that wafted through the air when she walked by. He'd take raspberry any day over coffee and breakfast.

When his eyes grew weary of reading, he glanced up to study her. He liked her short hair. On some women, the sticking out all over stuff would have looked unkempt, but not Rachel. She looked fresh and vibrant, reminding him of a little girl inside a woman's body.

Whoa, boy, he thought, forcing his attention back to his notes. *Those are dangerous thoughts. Your feelings must be coming from some protective instinct or a desire to help the underdog.* Since childhood, Adam always aided those with odds against them—like stray animals and the kids others picked on. Tutoring wasn't new to him either. He'd done it since high school. Whatever the explanation, Adam found himself knee deep in Rachel Morton's charms.

Frustrated with his thoughts, Adam attempted to reason with his emotions. He didn't have time for anyone or anything else in his life. He'd be busy for the next several years raising Bud. Why would he want to become involved with a woman and three more children? He downed his coffee, paid his bill, and hurried to the office.

seven

Saturday night came all too quickly as far as Rachel was concerned. She didn't know which threatened her more: having Adam help her prepare for the placement test or talking to Bud. She learned one important factor in talking with those who had problems with their lifestyle—be a friend first and earn their trust. That came as a priority. Once she secured Bud's trust, then she could give him her testimony. That part too was always difficult. Transparency came with a cost. Sometimes those she attempted to counsel rejected her because of her past mistakes.

Rachel stood in front of Adam's apartment door and rang the doorbell. From the way her knees knocked, he probably thought she'd pounded on the door too. In the next moment, he opened the door. She'd been accustomed to seeing him in a suit and wingtips, and viewing him for the first time in jeans and a T-shirt startled her.

"Have I grown horns?" he asked with a grin.

"No, not at all." *Rachel, stop stammering.* "I expected you to be in a suit." She laughed at how ridiculous she sounded.

"Do you want me to change?" His teasing eased her ruffled nerves a little, but she'd already decided the evening stretched beyond her comfort zone.

"No, Silly. I'm merely adjusting my eyes," she replied.

"Come on in. I'm ready to take on the world tonight."

One step at a time. My stomach is fluttering like a hundred hatched butterflies. "Let's hope that includes helping me pass my test. Here." She handed him a to-go bag from the restaurant. "I brought a couple of pieces of Joan's triple-fudge cookie pie."

Adam grimaced. "Since I took you on as a client, I've gained five pounds."

50

"I can return it or give both to Bud." She bit her lip to keep from laughing.

"Absolutely not." He took the bag and called for Bud. "We have dessert."

While Adam and Bud inhaled the chocolate pie, Rachel noted the fondness Adam and Bud showed for each other. The boy looked much better—rested, better color in his skin. . .and hair—and certainly in a better mood.

"How's your uncle treating you?" she asked, resting her arms on the table.

Bud shrugged. "Okay, except for doing homework, going to school, taking showers, getting to bed early, no junk food, church—"

"Hey, isn't there anything good about living with me?" Adam managed a hurtful tone.

Bud pointed to Rachel. "Tutoring Rachel and having her bring pie."

Adam palmed his hand against his forehead. "See what my life is like, Rachel? It's a wonder I can even function."

She laughed. "In the future, remind me to bring sweet treats."

"Right now," Adam said, pushing back an empty plate, "we need to get busy. Bud, you head back to your room for homework. I'll quiz you later."

Bud uttered a groan. "Uncle Adam."

"I know it's Saturday and you helped me all day at the farm, but I wanted us to drive to Austin tomorrow afternoon and take in a movie and dinner." He turned to Rachel. "We have work to do."

Bud scraped his finger along the plate, gathering up the last crumbs of the pie, and poked it in his mouth. "Watch his whip," he warned.

Rachel opened her notebook. "I'm ready."

Adam handed her the day's newspaper. "Let's start with you reading this short article, then I'll ask questions."

Rachel took a deep breath and hoped Adam didn't see her trembling. He turned the paper toward her and pointed to an article about a high school play.

"I'll give you about five minutes while I check on Bud's status. He has a tendency to flip on the TV and forget about school work."

The article could have been written in Greek or Latin for all Rachel knew. She read it three times before Adam returned.

"Let's see what you remember," he said.

"Not much, Adam. I'm terribly nervous."

"Ah, I bet you'll surprise yourself. The article was about a play given by the local high school. What was the name of the play?"

"*Beauty and the Beast.*" She folded her hands and placed them on her lap.

He smiled. "When is the performance?"

She didn't remember the dates, but she assumed a weekend. "I could guess, but that's not what I should do."

"Do you remember the price of the tickets?"

"Five dollars for students and ten for adults."

Adam nodded. "See, your comprehension's not so bad."

"Yeah, but the reason I remembered was I thought my kids would enjoy it."

"It doesn't matter how you remembered, but that you did."

She felt herself flush.

"Do you remember any of the actors or actresses?"

Rachel moistened her lips and thought hard. "No."

"Uncle Adam, what is 'x' in the equation, 'x' plus the remainder of twenty minus eight equals forty?"

"Thirty-two." Rachel grimaced. "I'm sorry. Guess he needs to figure it out."

Adam rested his chin on his palm. "How did you get that so fast? He'd barely spoken the words, and you nailed him with the answer."

"Easy doing math in my head," she said. "It's doing the steps on paper where I have problems."

"Hey, Rachel, come on back and give me a hand," Bud called. "I have a few problems done, but I need to know if the answers are right."

"Go ahead," Adam whispered.

Rachel scooted back her chair and moved toward Bud's room. To her surprise, the boy's bedroom didn't have near the clutter and smell she associated with a boy. Although the room was small, a twin bed, dresser, desk, and chair fit quite nicely. She wondered what Rocky's room would be like in a few years. Would he be neat or messy?

She quickly answered Bud's questions and set him to work in figuring out the two wrong problems. Glancing about the room, she saw baseball posters above his head.

"Are you the baseball fan, or is that your uncle's decor?" she asked.

"Mine, but we both picked them out." Bud resembled Adam. In fact, the two could have passed for father and son. His natural, walnut-colored hair looked a whole lot better than the colors he'd been using the first time she saw him. "We're going to a game in Houston as soon as the season starts."

She walked over to one of the posters featuring the Houston Astros. "Your uncle must care a whole lot about you."

"More than my dad, and my mom left us last year."

"Sorry to hear that."

Bud shrugged. "Dad doesn't care what I do, but Uncle Adam is hard on me. I'd rather be with my friends."

"And what do your friends do?"

He turned to look at her. "Are you a school counselor or something?"

Rachel had to laugh with his question. "Not exactly. I've made a few bad choices in my life, and I hate to see anyone else do the same."

Bud stiffened. "I don't want anyone telling me what to do, so if my uncle sent you in here, there's the door."

Rachel wasn't about to be put off easily. She'd bent words with the worst of them, and at his age, she could upset her mother in ten seconds. "What does it matter either way? Wouldn't you rather have someone care than someone who just wants you out of sight?"

"I said I want to be left alone." Bud rose from his chair. "I need a cigarette and a beer," he said. "If you can't get them for me, get out of my room."

Rachel crossed her arms. She knew Adam was listening to every word. "You don't shock me in the least. I've seen girls a lot tougher than you."

"Oh yeah." The hostility that she'd seen in the restaurant surfaced. "What do you know?"

She raised a brow and looked over Bud's head to see Adam in the background. Fury etched across his face. She ignored him and turned her attention back to the boy before her. "Tell you what I know." She uncrossed her arms and planted her hands on the desk in front of the boy. "You think you're tough by wanting a cigarette and a beer? I know where to get every drug you can possibly think of. I know what it costs and the best price. I know how to get hold of guys who would smash your face just for kicks. I've been in jail more times than I care to remember, and I've done time in prison, and let me tell you Mr. Bud, none of it is worth it."

"I don't believe a word." Bud threw his words at her like dumping trash.

"That's your choice." Rachel pointed to the other room. "Ask your uncle, he'll tell you. But when you're ready to give up that attitude, come talk to me."

She gave him a nod and left the room, closing the door behind her. Down the hallway, Adam waited. If the color of his face and the set of his jaw were any indication of his blood pressure, he needed a doctor.

"I did some tutoring," she said. "Who are you upset with, Bud or me?"

Adam leaned against the kitchen counter and shook his head. "Now, how could I be angry at you? You come over here expecting me to help you with placement tests, and instead I throw you into a den of lions."

"One little cub," she said, drawing out each word. "And I'm

quite capable of taking care of myself—in most instances."

A lock of dark hair fell on Adam's forehead. His dark blue eyes peered into hers, capturing her gaze and holding her captive. "I think you handled yourself very well," he said. "But right now, I'm going to make him apologize."

She stepped closer. "He wouldn't mean it, and what is a forced apology? I'd rather he come to me when he feels remorse in his heart. I wasn't all sweet and nice either."

"You told him the truth."

"He needs to hear it." She hesitated and braved forward. "He has an edge on you, because you don't know his world. You're educated, professional, a role model, a Christian, and a source of security. He doesn't have any of those things at home, and he's not so sure he needs or wants them. My guess is he's hurting and lashing out by putting on this gang-like facade. Unfortunately, he's not too young to get started in that lifestyle."

"That's what I'm afraid of," Adam said. "On behalf of my nephew, I am sorry for the things he said."

"No problem." She walked to the table and picked up her notebook. Their hour had slipped by and she needed to get home. "May I ask you a question?"

"Sure."

"Remember when you asked me questions about my kids, things I needed to determine?" When he said yes, she continued. "Do you love Bud? Because if you've taken him on as an obligation or a responsibility, he'll see right through you."

He gave her a tight-lipped smile. "I do. From the time he was born, I've loved him like he was my own, which is one of the reasons why this is tearing me apart."

"If you don't already, tell him. Tell him often." Rachel picked up her purse and the notepad.

"Any charge for tonight?" he asked in a tone she'd learned to recognize as an inching toward humor.

"My secretary will bill you."

"We didn't make much progress in preparing you for the

placement test." Adam's words were soft, not at all the self-confident attorney-at-law.

"Everything takes time."

"I can see that."

Rachel released a sigh and turned for the door. Adam stepped in front of her.

"Thank you for tonight," he said. "I'll continue to do all I can to help you gain custody of your children."

She felt the familiar warmth wind through her body. He stood too close to her, and it almost frightened her. "Whether we're successful or not, I will forever be grateful for what you've done to help me."

Adam reached for the door and opened it into the apartment hallway. "Have a good evening, Rachel. I'll. . ."

She studied his face, but he never finished the sentence. Something in his eyes stopped her, something woven with warmth and sincerity. His eyes softened. Without another word, she left, wondering what exactly happened in those last few moments in Adam Raeburn's apartment.

eight

Adam waited several minutes before he walked back to Bud's bedroom. Anger at the boy's behavior surfaced repeatedly. He wanted to throttle the kid in one breath and hug him in the next. Adam realized he needed to settle his anger before talking to his nephew. Without that control, Adam presented no more of a role model than Rob or Millie.

Lord, please give me the words. Bud is worse than I thought.

Dark shadows settled as he made the trek to the boy's door. Odd, he hadn't noticed the length before. Just as he lifted his hand to knock, an inner voice stopped him. He reached up again, but the same sensation told him to leave the boy alone. The direction made no sense. If Adam planned to assume the parental role, then this situation must be addressed. Not understanding why, Adam retraced his steps to the kitchen.

Totally helpless, he wished Rachel hadn't left. She'd gently handled Bud's smart mouth where Adam would have blown up. He'd invited her this evening to help with the placement test and possibly offer some encouragement to Bud, not to handle his nephew's impertinent behavior.

Adam recalled how Rachel had interacted with Bud all evening. She'd been a friend and a counselor—and she had empathy for his mistakes. Taking a deep breath, Adam considered his commitment to help Rachel reach her goals. Not only had he done little to aid in the endeavor, but he'd also failed to schedule another session. Adam wondered if the whole problem behind her inability to take tests lay in her overpowering mother. From what he'd learned about Thelma Myers, she possessed a critical tongue and expected perfection from people. Rachel's situation could have resulted from fear of disappointing her mother. The circumstances could have led to Rachel's mental paralysis and her resulting lack of self-confidence. Adam's theory made perfect sense to him, and he'd discussed it with Greg. In fact, his pastor planned to delicately bring up the matter in one of Rachel's upcoming counseling sessions. Certainly tonight had proved Rachel had a quick mind for math—and a host of other things. A lot of wisdom rested inside her pretty head.

Adam snatched up his cell phone and walked onto his balcony. By now he had Rachel's number memorized, and the thought brought a stark realization to his mind. She meant more to him in this short time than a normal client to an attorney. She answered on the second ring.

"Rachel, this is Adam."

"Is anything wrong with Bud?"

"I don't think so. I haven't tried talking to him."

"You're probably wise. He may need time to think about what happened between us. I'm sorry. You called me. What do you need?"

Seeing more of you, for starters. "I neglected to schedule another tutoring session."

Rachel sighed. "I really need to work tomorrow and for the next several days."

"What about before church tomorrow morning? I believe you're attending the second service because of your children's visit. Are you in Sunday school?"

"Yes, right before worship."

Adam considered his own busy morning. "Could we meet as early as seven o'clock? For about an hour in the sanctuary? I can then swing back home for Bud."

"I–I believe seven is fine. Adam, you don't have to do this."

"I want to. It's good for my ego." He laughed, then sobered. "I know your placement tests have nothing to do with the custody hearing, but as I may have said before, the testing does impact your future."

A moment of silence passed between them.

"Thanks, Adam. You're a true friend, and I appreciate all you do."

The conversation ended, leaving Adam wanting to hear her sweet voice for awhile longer. Sticking the phone in his rear jean pocket, he gazed out over the neighborhood beneath a navy blue sky and watched the house lights flicker on. Children laughed. A woman shouted for her boys to get inside and take a bath—tomorrow was a church day. A man whistled, then called for his dog, a door slammed, and a horn tooted.

A home of his own danced across Adam's mind. *A home with a family.* This deep desire had led him to purchase seventy acres and a nineteenth-century farmhouse right outside of Brenham. Adam laughed in remembering the Realtor's description of the home that had "decorator appeal." The woodwork still had the original varnish, and most of the floors were hardwood. While staring up at the tall ceilings and admiring the hand-carved molding, he gave in and made an offer on the spot.

In short, everything in the house needed to be redone, but Adam couldn't resist the challenge. Picturesque hills rounded the view from a kitchen window. A winding creek flowed midway through the acreage, and a stocked catfish pond had him yearning for a fishing pole. The house sat beneath century-old oaks, and the backyard sent a nostalgic message welcoming others to a less complicated lifestyle. The stone-and-wood home had held his attention every Saturday since he'd taken possession a few months ago. New plumbing and wiring brought it up to building codes. A dilapidated front porch with a sagging roof and rotted flooring were replaced and a swing added. Later on, closets were carved out of the huge bedrooms and three-and-a-half baths added for convenience. The outhouse had charm, but the combination of inconvenience and wasp nests didn't fit into his wants or needs.

Ushering in the present, a niggling thought assaulted him. What would he do once the house was restored and remodeled? Live in it with Bud? Adam had already drawn up the paperwork for permanent custody, and Rob had signed them. Along with everything else, this last stunt of Bud going to school drunk proved Rob had no control over his son.

"I'm heading to Florida, and Millie's already left for New York," Rob had said. "Everything here is depressing, and I don't plan to ever come back—nothing good to come back to."

Rob had no idea what he was throwing away—a human being who desperately craved guidance. Adam ached with love for his nephew, who had been tossed and hurt like a stray cat. With those admissions, Adam wanted brothers and sisters for Bud. More importantly, Adam wanted a wife who loved both of them despite their faults.

He'd prayed for such a woman over the past six years, and to date no woman even tempted him. That is, until he met Rachel. What at first appeared as the most unlikely wife material on the face of the earth, now impressed him with her gentleness and wisdom. Rachel Morton. No one would have ever paired the two of them, but, then again, God did strange and wondrous things. Observing her with Bud tonight led Adam to believe she'd do a marvelous job at mothering. If he took the time to list her attributes after such a few short weeks, he'd have a dissertation. Imagine what six months, six years, or sixty years might bring.

Adam wanted the kind of Christian marriage he'd seen in his parents; in the couple who owned a bed-and-breakfast adjoining his land, Rick and Paula Davenport; and in Pastor Johnston and his wife.

What am I doing contemplating marriage to a woman I barely know? Adam swallowed hard at the idea creeping into his mind. A scary sensation wiggled through his body. What did he know about raising children? For that matter, what did he know about being a husband?

Adam's mind shouted at him to abort all thoughts about Rachel except her custody hearing and placement tests into college. His musings were premature and way out of line. Once he completed the class on stress management, his life would hold more control, and these far-fetched ideas would fade away.

Rachel listened to the organist quietly practice for the morning's service. Sitting alone in the worship center made her feel incredibly small and yet incredibly loved. A powerful and unique whirl of peace settled on her shoulders. She closed her eyes and allowed the feeling to warm her through and through. Prayer and praise poured from her soul. She wasn't asking for anything; God knew her heart. She simply lingered in the moment, like resting in a hot bubble bath after a wearisome day—only better.

A few moments later, events and conversations flooded her brain until she gave them to the Great Counselor. Autumn, Summer, Rocky, Mom and Dad, Bud, school, the future, and Adam tapped into her reservoir of burdens. Her prayers for that person or situation immediately soared skyward, except when she touched on Adam.

She recalled the look that passed between them last night. Was she being overly sensitive, or did she see something in his eyes indicating he might think of her as more than a client?

Of course not, you silly girl. No man in his right mind dare consider the likes of her and three troubled children. Well, foolishness had definitely set in. She asked God to forgive her inappropriate notions. Considering a possible relationship with Adam insulted him worse than throwing a bucket of ice water into his face. A man as fine as Adam Raeburn deserved a woman who matched his intellect and walk with the Lord.

"Good morning." Adam's voice barely registered over the soft strains of the organ. "Am I interrupting anything?"

"Just basking." She patted the cushioned pew for him to sit. All the while she considered the embarrassment of Adam discovering her deepest ponderings. She lifted her notebook beneath her Bible. "So what is on your syllabus today?"

"Basically talk. The more I think about what you attempted to do for my nephew last night, the more I am indebted."

"You? Really, Adam, I'm the charity case here."

"Let me remind you of my nephew who desperately needs a little understanding and a dose of reality."

"I'm sure a licensed counselor could do wonders for him."

"I'm more inclined to believe someone with a little empathy and—excuse me for saying this—experience can help more."

She shrugged. "Experience I certainly have."

"One other thing here. I'm suggesting heavy doses of prayer to help you through the placement tests. I believe your problem is more confidence than lack of knowledge. I want to help you prepare, but I don't believe the problem is as serious as you may think."

"You've already figured out I have no self-confidence." Her attention focused on the cross behind the choir loft.

"All right, I'll prove it in a series of questions. You don't have to answer, just listen. Joan states you run the restaurant as well if not better than she does. How many wait-staff are needed on a Saturday morning versus a Saturday night? What is the approximate amount of fresh produce needed per week? What is the temperature of the oil to cook chicken-fried steak, French fries, or catfish? How long is a customer expected to wait for his meal? When you first meet a customer, what is the biggest factor in determining how much tip he'll leave, if any? And my final question: Which is cheaper for Joan—lots of help working part-time or fewer people working full-time? And why?"

Rachel laughed.

"You knew those answers without thinking," Adam said.

"But it's my job."

"It's confidence in your job. I have an idea what's on the test. Most people have problems with the math and others with English. I think you will ace them both." He took on a serious demeanor. "Do I make you nervous?"

She slid a glance his way. Rachel still had her pride. "Lawyers used to take turns mopping the floor with me. Of course, I gave them plenty of reasons to do so."

"The first time we met I was horrible."

"But you've turned into a rather nice guy." *Watch yourself, Rachel.*

Adam drummed his fingers on his Bible. "Then, are we still friends?"

"Mortal enemies."

"For how long?"

"At least thirty more seconds."

He pulled back the cuff on his shirt and stared at his watch. "Twenty-nine, twenty-eight, twenty-seven. . ."

❧

Adam watched Rachel with her children in the foyer. He appreciated the way she gave each one individual attention, sincere kindness, and no partiality. Rocky shared in his sisters' looks—dark hair, light olive skin, and those incredible green eyes.

Adam cringed. The oldest little girl turned away from Rachel's attention, but Rachel remained in control. He'd heard the passion in her voice when she spoke about her children. He understood how deeply she hurt.

His attention focused on Archie and Thelma Myers. Archie wrapped his arms around Rachel's shoulders and pressed a kiss against her cheek. Thelma was another matter. She gave her daughter a thin-lipped smile and held onto Autumn's hand. Adam deliberated on Thelma for a moment. According to Greg and Rachel, a massive heart attack changed her disposition, but viewing her with Rachel put him in mind of the old Thelma. She probably hurt too. Her daughter had disappointed and humiliated her, and she'd taken her grandchildren as atonement. Now, Rachel wanted her kids back, and the grandmother didn't particularly like the idea. If Adam considered the matter, he doubted if Rachel had told her parents about the custody suit.

Adam couldn't blame Thelma. From the sound of things, she had been through a war with her daughter. Any trust most likely had vanished when Rachel went to prison. How many times had he told Bud that trust had to be earned? Adam's gaze swept to Autumn's face again. Without a doubt, the little girl modeled her hurt and resentment the same way as Grandma. He couldn't blame any of them, not really. The underlying issue here lay in what was best for the children: grandparents who loved and took the utmost care of their grandchildren or the mother who struggled to exist but loved them equally as much?

"I'm ready to go," Bud said. Already his shirt trailed outside his jeans, and his facial expression read boredom.

"Sure. Want to catch a burger somewhere?"

"Yeah, I'm starved. Why are you staring at Rachel?"

Adam swung a glance at his nephew. "I'm not. I'm admiring her children."

"Right. I see the way you look at her, and it's not her kids you're hung up on." Bud smirked, and the look irritated Adam.

"She's a client. Anything else is unprofessional."

Bud shrugged. "Rachel won't always be your client."

If Bud sensed Adam's feelings, then did anyone else? "Let's go. I'm not in the mood to argue."

The two headed through the door and out into the brisk weather. The slight chill felt refreshing. Adam and Bud walked toward the car in silence.

"I'd rather have pizza," Bud said.

"Sounds good to me. Do you want to see your dad?"

"Nope. I'd rather spend the entire day helping you strip floors again." Bud laughed, the first time since the past Saturday night. "She is pretty," he added.

Adam thought he might as well humor the kid. It sure kept the peace. And he'd heard some of the terms guys used to describe attractive women. Bud's description meant Rachel had his respect. "Who?"

"Rachel. Don't play dumb, Uncle Adam. Hey, were all those things she said to me true?"

"Unfortunately, yes. She had quite a colorful past until she turned to the Lord."

Bud shook his head. "Here she is in church."

"Gives you something to think about, doesn't it?" Adam

asked. "Say, what was your Sunday school lesson about?"

"Ah, I bet you don't think I listened, but I did. It was about Peter's dream when God said all food was clean when what He really meant was Jesus had come to earth for everyone."

"I'm impressed."

"Well, it made me think of Rachel."

Thanks, Lord. I think we're getting somewhere. "Explain yourself."

"Some folks think Jesus is just for those people who never get into trouble." Bud sighed. "Uncle Adam, am I going back to my dad's?"

"Do you want to?"

"Are you kidding? You might not believe this, but he gave me beer. Said I'd sleep better."

Anger swelled in Adam. "Rob loves you the best way he can, and you will always owe him respect. The Bible says that." He paused. "I might as well come clean. I've filed for permanent custody."

"Then we'll be a family?" Bud's earnest face brought back all the memories of the toddler who used to follow him around asking for "Unkie Adam."

"Looks that way. I thought we'd move to the farm as soon as it's done." Adam wondered if he'd said too much. His legal mind wrestled with the love he held for the boy. Adam wanted to protect Bud from his father's world.

"Cool. Once you marry Rachel, we'll be a great family."

nine

Rachel studied Rocky sitting next to her. His flushed face and the way he picked at his food bothered her. Rocky had an appetite that rivaled both of his sisters put together. He seemed whiney too.

"Rocky, do you feel bad?" she whispered.

The little boy peered up and tears filled his dark eyes. "My ear hurts."

"Oh, Honey, I'm so sorry." Rachel glanced at her mom. "Rocky is complaining of an earache. Do you have any Children's Tylenol?"

"He mentioned it yesterday evening. He'd been cranky, and I gave him a timeout thinking it was an excuse for bad behavior," her mother said.

Rachel touched his forehead. "He's burning up. We need to take him to the emergency room."

Mom scooted back her chair and stood. "We will take care of his medical needs. Don't you need to be at work?"

Rachel clenched her fist and smiled in a desperate measure not to lose control. "Yes, I do, but Rocky's health comes first."

"Since when does anything about these children matter to you?"

Her mother's tone pierced Rachel's heart. Why must everything be such an uphill battle? "Since I turned over my life to Jesus two years ago," Rachel said more calmly than she felt. Rocky began to whimper. "Do you want Mommy to hold you?" she asked.

He shook his head and reached for her mother. "I want Grandma."

Rachel attempted to swallow the pain searing her heart like

66

a hot poker. Tears pooled in her eyes, and she hastily blinked them back.

Mom lifted Rocky into her arms. His legs kicked at the glass of milk beside his plate, and the contents spilled into Rachel's lap. She snatched up her cloth napkin and soaked up the milk on her skirt.

"He knows who takes the best care of him," her mother said. Rocky laid his head on Mom's shoulder as if he were a baby again. "Grandma will take care of you, Darlin'. Certainly not an only-on-Sunday mother."

Rachel held her breath. Stunned, she couldn't believe the words from Mom's mouth—and in front of the children. What else had she said to them?

"Thelma, you've said enough," Archie said. "We'll talk later." He turned to Autumn and Summer. "Girls, we need to leave. Your little brother is sick and needs a doctor."

"I'd like to go with you." Rachel rose from the table and pulled back Summer's chair.

"It's not necessary." Mom lifted her chin. "We can manage without you. We've done fine in the past."

"Thelma." Dad's voice rose. "There's no reason to talk to Rachel this way."

"I'm merely pointing out facts and reality," Mom replied.

"Can you tell me where you're taking him?" At that moment, Rachel would have fallen on her knees and begged.

Mom refused eye contact. "I don't know for sure. Maybe the clinic, maybe the emergency room, or maybe I'll call his pediatrician and explain the situation."

A knife twisted in Rachel's stomach. "Are you going home then?"

"I haven't decided."

Dad cleared his throat. "Rachel deserves to know what is happening to her son."

"She has no rights, Archie. Remember, she lost them." With those words flung like grenades, Mom started for the door. Autumn trailed behind her.

"I want you, Mommy," Summer said. "I don't care what they say. I love you."

Rachel bent and hugged the little girl. "I love you too."

"Can't we be together all the time?"

Determination braced Rachel before she burst into tears and said hurtful things about her mother. "I'd like nothing better than to be with you and your sister and brother, but for now things will have to be like this."

Summer clung to her, sobbing. Rachel glanced up at her dad and silently begged for help. He pried the little girl from Rachel's waist and scooped her up into his arms.

"I'm sorry, Honey." He handed Rachel money. "Would you take care of the check?"

She nodded and her lips quivered.

"I don't know what's wrong with your mother," he said. "She's not sleeping for some reason. It's like she used to be before—"

"You're the one who always said there were no excuses for bad behavior," Rachel said, fighting the urge to pick up one of the chairs and send it across the room.

He touched her cheek. "I love you, Sweetheart. This will all work out for the best, God's best. I'll call you as soon as I find out about Rocky."

"Thanks, Dad."

He touched Rachel's back and planted a kiss on her forehead.

"You know I've started to do something about this."

He nodded. "How soon?"

"Two months."

"This is horrible for all of us. I know you love your children, but so do we."

"Dad, please believe me. I want what God desires, whatever that may be."

Rachel cried all the way back to her car. Deep, wrenching sobs shook her body as she drove down the street. She steered her old car into the parking lot of a convenience store and turned off the engine. The tears refused to stop. Her children were her life. She wanted a chance to make up for all the mistakes from the past. Did God really care? Did she really want what was best for them?

I want Grandma. Rocky's words tore through her mind, each time a little louder than the time before.

She understood the attachment between her children and their grandparents. Mom and Dad had given them a home and an abundance of love. Naturally, the three children would look to their grandparents for security. Today should have been no surprise, but recognizing the truth didn't make the pain go away.

I am a poor mother. Look what I did to those poor babies. I deserted them for a man who cared more about the next high than he did for his family.

Rachel wanted to remember Scripture and find comfort in God's promises. The passages refused to come. All she could think about was her own guilt and shame, although she knew those accusations didn't come from God. This must be the answer. Her heavenly Father wanted the children with their grandparents. Today had to be an answer to prayer; no matter if she couldn't bear or accept it.

I don't even have the sense to help them with their homework.

"Can't you ever just learn something without all of this trouble?" her mother had asked years ago. "You could do anything you want, if you'd put your mind to it. You're lazy, Rachel. You'll never amount to anything." How profound, Rachel thought. Dear Mom had been right.

Accepting the inevitable, Rachel climbed out of her car and headed toward the pay phone. Right now, before she lost courage, she'd call Adam and ask him to drop the proceedings. What did she have to offer Autumn, Summer, and Rocky but a mother with a troubled past?

Rachel pulled a tissue from her purse and blew her nose before phoning Adam. She hoped he wouldn't be annoyed with her calling on Sunday. With a deep breath, she pressed in the cell number on his business card. He answered on the third ring.

"Hi, Adam. This is Rachel. I apologize for this interruption to your Sunday afternoon, but I wanted to let you know that you're off the hook."

"What do you mean?" Adam's voice was laden with concern. "What's wrong? You sound upset."

"I'm fine. Uh, I've decided the children are better off with my parents."

"You didn't sound that way this morning. What happened during lunch?" he asked.

Rachel closed her eyes, then braved forward. "Oh, this decision didn't come about today. I've been thinking about it for quite awhile."

"I think something happened at lunch."

She said nothing—not wanting to lie, but refusing to tell the truth either.

"Rachel, I can't help you if you don't talk."

"You've helped enough. Now you can go back to accepting real clients who pay real money."

"Are you feeling sorry for yourself, Rachel?"

His question lit a match under her emotions. "How dare you ask such a question? I'm acting on behalf of the welfare of my children. My parents can give them more than I ever could."

"Are you at home?"

She hated being ignored. "No, I'm outside a convenience store." She suddenly remembered. "Adam, I forgot. You and Bud are on your way to Austin."

"We changed our minds—too tired to make the drive. Now where are you?"

"It doesn't matter, Adam. I'm on my way home to change clothes and get to work by three-thirty."

"That means you have an hour and a half."

She glanced at her watch. "To do what? Sign paperwork to cancel our business association?"

"No, for me to talk to you face-to-face about this."

Rachel groaned. "I refuse to have a single man in my apartment. Can you imagine what that would look like to everyone who is looking for me to make more mistakes?"

"Fine," Adam said. "I'll wait on the sidewalk outside your building. I know exactly where it is—the corner of East Main and Market. And if you don't show up, I'll throw rocks at your windows."

"You wouldn't." Anger simmered just below the boiling point.

"Try me. As your attorney who refuses to give up on this case, I plan to be in front of your apartment in exactly fifteen minutes. I suggest you hurry home and get changed for work."

Rachel heard the click of Adam ending the call. This conversation hadn't ended the way she'd envisioned. Things rarely did.

❦

Adam shielded his eyes from the glaring sun and stared up at the second story of the turn-of-the-century brick building. The bottom floor housed a coffee and pastry shop, and Rachel lived in one of the apartments above it. He'd give her five more minutes before he climbed the stairs and started banging on doors.

Hearing a door slam, he swung his gaze to the left where a yellow-uniformed young woman hurried down the steps. Grinning, Adam bent down and picked up a couple of stones.

"A little more, and you'd be hearing me ping your windows," he said, but his words trailed off at the look on her face. Her swollen eyes and puffy face told the truth. "Oh, Rachel, what is wrong?"

The moment he captured her attention, her green eyes pooled. Blinking them back, she hastily looked away.

"Rachel."

"Adam, I don't know if I can talk without crying. This afternoon has been hard." Her lips quivered, and an overwhelming urge to wrap his arms around her nearly took control.

"Tell me what happened, and I'll help you work through it."

"No matter what you say, it won't change my mind. I'm dropping the custody hearing."

"What ruined lunch with your kids?"

Rachel glanced around while an elderly couple walked by. "The truth."

"I can call your dad."

She glared at him. "No, please, I'll tell you. I was seated between Rocky and Summer when I noticed Rocky picking at his food. He didn't look well, so I asked him if he felt bad. He complained of an earache." She stopped and took a deep breath. "Rocky wanted my mother, not me. Then Mom let me know that she and Dad are the guardians and reminded me of my lack of mothering skills. I wanted to follow them to a clinic or wherever she planned to take Rocky, but Mom refused. Dad took up for me, which didn't help. To top things off, Summer got upset."

Anger mounted in Adam. "Are you telling me that your parents took your son for medical help and you have no idea where?"

Rachel nodded and blinked again. "I was furious, but I didn't say a word. I did tell Dad that I had started to do something about the children. He looked devastated. Then I began to really think about the situation."

She looked into Adam's face. "My folks are the best ones to raise my children. They have the funds, both are Christian role models, and they care about those kids. I'm being incredibly selfish by fighting for custody."

In the beginning Adam had wondered the same thing, but the longer he spent time with Rachel, the more he realized the depth of her love for them.

"Have you talked to God about this?" he asked.

"Many, many times. The truth is, if I look at the situation realistically, my parents are the better choice."

"In whose eyes?"

She hesitated. "You know I love them."

"Then fight for them."

Rachel crossed her arms over her chest. The air had grown cooler, and she didn't have a jacket or a sweater. He removed his lightweight jacket and draped it over her shoulders. He lifted her chin with his fingertip.

"Every child deserves a loving and devoted mother. Neither

of those requirements involves a large bank roll, only a large heart. You can do this, Rachel. Let those of us who care help you through it."

"But my own baby didn't want me, and my mother believes I've not left the past behind."

"Then we must prove her wrong."

A car pulled next to the curb, and Rachel hurried to the driver's side. Archie Myers rolled down his window.

"Rocky has an ear infection," he said. "The doctor at the clinic gave him a shot and a prescription. He did have a fever, but that will come down with Children's Tylenol."

"Thanks for coming by to tell me."

"Nothing would have stopped me."

She pressed her lips together. "Guess I need to get to work."

Archie nodded, and Rachel hurried back to Adam.

"I heard the news," Adam said. "I'm glad he's going to be okay." He looked at his watch. "How about I walk you to work?"

"I—I'd like that, but I haven't changed my mind."

"Will you wait until tomorrow to make a final decision?" Adam asked. "Everything looks better in the morning."

She turned to walk toward the restaurant, and he joined her. "All right. I'll pray about it one more time."

"Atta girl. Will you call me first thing in the morning?"

She closed her eyes. "I suppose. I have to work breakfast through dinner, but I'll get a break before lunch."

They walked on toward the restaurant's entrance. She slipped his jacket from her shoulders and offered a word of thanks. "You'll need this. It's a bit chilly."

"What about when you're finished with work tonight?" He could see her rushing home in the cold.

"I'll be fine."

"I think not. You keep the jacket, and I'll be back here to walk you home. I don't like the idea of your walking home alone at night."

Rachel smiled. "Another part of your job?"

Adam's heart pounded like a drum. "No, this is all me."

She tilted her head and studied him curiously. "I'm not so sure I understand."

"I don't either, not exactly."

Her face reddened, and he realized he'd said more than he should. "You're a sweet lady, and I hate to see you upset and struggling on your own, especially when I can help."

Suddenly Rachel whipped around. "I am not a charity case, Adam. I've told you that before. Don't feel sorry for me. I made my choices and I'm paying for them. But don't ever—"

She stopped on the sidewalk and faced him squarely. "Don't treat me like some lost puppy whose destiny is the dog pound. I managed fine without you, and I'll manage fine again. I won't be needing your legal services or your sympathy."

ten

Two and a half hours later, the scene at lunch with her family then the scene with Adam replayed in Rachel's mind. Her mother didn't believe she'd changed at all and refused to allow her to accompany her own son to the doctor. Rocky needed his mother today, not his grandmother. All of her children needed their mother. And to make matters worse, Adam didn't understand how she felt.

The entire situation left her tired, angry, and hurt. She wanted to see a way out of this mess, but she didn't even see a light. Every day began with a struggle, and every night ended the same. At times she wondered why she tried to make any sense of life at all.

"What's wrong, Rachel?" Joan asked while Rachel filled glasses with iced tea for her table. "You're smiling, you're going through the motions of a great waitress, but I see something in your eyes that words and actions can't mask. Not to mention the swollen eyes I noticed when you came in this afternoon."

"Bad day. I'll be fine."

"Didn't you have lunch with your parents and children?" Joan asked.

"Yes, Ma'am."

"It must not have gone well."

"No, it didn't. Rocky had. . ." Rachel spilled out the story as quickly as possible. "I'm furious at Mom and Adam. While Mom condemns me, Adam goes to the other extreme."

"Adam is your attorney, right?" Joan rested her hands on her ample hips. "I understand your frustration with your mother, but it sounds like your attorney is trying to help."

"More like he's trying to run my life," Rachel said, shaking her head.

Joan squeezed Rachel's waist. "Honey, I can see why you're hurt about Rocky's illness and your mother's words, but I don't see why Adam has you so upset."

Rachel started to state all of the reasons why the attorney infuriated her so, but stopped. "Are you kidding? He wants to dictate his opinion."

"Looks to me like he's doing all he can to help you get your kids back. Have you noticed how many times he's been in here since he took on your case? I'd say he's more than a little interested in his client."

Rachel's eyes widened. "Joan, you're very wrong. He's not interested in me." She glanced about the restaurant.

"Am I? Take a look in the mirror, Little Lady. You're beautiful from the inside out. God's love is radiating in your every breath. Mark my word, Adam Raeburn has taken notice."

"But I'm a—you know what I am, and look at all the things I've done. An educated, godly man would never give me a second look."

"If God throws our sins into the sea never to remember them again, then why wouldn't Adam Raeburn?" Joan punctuated her words with her finger on the countertop.

Rachel moistened her lips. She set the glass of iced tea onto the tray and clenched her fists a few times to stop the shaking. Could this be true? She remembered the look in Adam's eyes on more than one occasion—tender gazes that stunned her mind with forbidden dreams of a chance to have a good marriage and a wonderful father for her children.

Joan tilted her head and laughed. "I think you've noticed him too. Maybe what you feel today is more of an emotional confusion aimed at yourself than anger with Adam."

"I don't know what to do, Joan." Rachel couldn't reveal her heart, but she could admit she'd overreacted today. "I need to apologize to Adam."

"Sounds like an excellent idea to me. And you're not dropping the custody suit, or I will take over the role of your mother."

"You already have." She smiled. "I will finish what I

started and let God decide what is best for the kids. When I'm finished tonight, I'll make amends."

Joan crossed her arms. "You don't have to wait until you're off work." She pointed to the door. "He's just arrived with his nephew."

Rachel swung her gaze around. Adam waved as though nothing had happened. *And I thought God was the Relentless Pursuer. Looks like Adam has been taking lessons.* She waved back, wondering if Joan could be right. No matter how perfect her dear friend's observations sounded, nothing could happen between her and Adam. Maybe in the future when she had her children, a college degree, and a good relationship with her mother, things might be different. Right now, she had to walk this journey alone.

She studied Bud. Adam had his hands full with one twelve year old. He didn't need four more needy people to add to the collection.

❧

Adam watched Rachel serve an adjoining table. "Hi, Adam. Hi, Bud. I'll be with you in a minute." She smiled—rather stiffly, but a smile nevertheless.

"Take your time." Adam questioned whether this was the same woman who didn't need his legal advice or sympathy. It hadn't been three hours since she led him to believe he was at the bottom of her friend list.

"Did you two have a fight?" Bud asked.

Adam slid a glare his way. "Whatever made you ask that?"

Bud stared down at his menu. "Because you remind me of a guy in my class who had a fight with his girlfriend."

Adam refused to believe he resembled a junior high kid. "You are dead wrong on this one. Rachel and I have a purely business relationship."

"Yeah, yeah. This guy I was just telling you about? He claimed he and this girl just did homework together."

"Please." Irritation crept through Adam's body.

Bud shrugged. "Suit yourself. I know what I see."

Adam decided not to pursue the topic, especially when Bud's perception nailed him. Coming here tonight for dinner might not have been a good idea after all. He thought seeing Rachel after she'd calmed down would have a positive effect on their relationship. The goal was to continue with the custody hearing. She'd had a bad day, and he'd been the one at whom she'd lashed out. She needed to see he had no hard feelings. The two had a professional relationship and nothing more.

He sighed and stole a sideways look at his nephew.

"One day you'll appreciate me." Bud grinned.

Rachel appeared with glasses of water. She avoided Adam's attention, took their drink and food orders, and disappeared.

"She's avoiding you." Bud took a long drink of water. "Do you want to talk about the problem? I have a good ear."

Adam nearly choked—from laughing. "Are you ready to hang out a shingle?"

"Sure. Adam Raeburn, attorney-at-law, and Bud Raeburn, counselor."

"Let's get you through the seventh grade first."

Adam felt certain the food was delicious, but his taste buds had taken a sabbatical. Rachel occupied more than one of his senses. He couldn't smell or hear either, except the raspberry scent that was so much a part of her. At one point, he dropped his fork twice; his sense of touch had taken a vacation.

Rachel smiled, laughed at Bud's antics, even inquired about Adam's afternoon—but nothing indicated she'd changed her mind about the custody hearing or their faltering friendship.

By the time he and Bud were finished eating, misery had its claws attached to Adam's heart. He handed Rachel payment for their meal and started to tell her to keep the change, but it occurred to him that since her tip would be generous, she might be angry all over again.

So he waited until she returned with the change. He rose from the table with thanks on his lips in hopes he'd catch her eye. He did.

"Do you have a minute to talk to me?" She looked much

more in control than he did, and her tone sounded pleasant. "Or should I call later?"

"What is best for you?" Adam asked.

"Miss, could we have more rolls, please?" an elderly man asked.

Rachel responded to the man, then focused her attention on Adam. "I guess I should call later."

Adam took a deep breath. "I'll be here at closing." He turned and left, not giving her a moment to refuse.

"You handled that well," Bud commented once they were outside the restaurant. "You don't want a woman to think she's in control."

"I'm glad I have your approval, but I don't agree with your reasoning." Adam decided breakfast or lunch were better times to talk to Rachel than with his highly observant nephew and his blunt advice. "God is the one in control—not a man or a woman."

"What about this submission stuff? I heard Pastor Johnston talking about a man being the head of his household and a woman doing what he says."

Give me a break! "You didn't hear the other side of it. God says a husband is to love his wife as Jesus loves the Church and gave His life for her. The Bible refers to the Church as Jesus' bride, and remember, He died for the Church. That's what a real husband is, Bud, a man who is willing to die for his wife."

Bud startled. "You made your point."

Promptly at ten o'clock that evening, after not being able to concentrate on anything productive, Adam parked in front of Rachel's apartment, then walked to the restaurant. He still wondered if she'd speak to him or if she planned on confirming her earlier plans to drop the case.

When Adam arrived, he instantly spotted Rachel wiping down tables. No customers lingered in the restaurant, so he seized the opportunity to meet her head on.

"May I help you?" He lifted salt and pepper shakers for her to clean beneath. He caught her smile and responded with one of his own.

"The job is a lot of hard work," she said.

"I can handle it." Adam's heart pounded, reminding him of the seventh grader Bud had mentioned.

"I can be difficult," she said, wiping off the chair seat where a child must have eaten.

"How difficult?" Adam moved the chair into place.

"I have temporary moments of near insanity."

He inwardly chuckled. "Describe them for me, if you don't mind. That will give me a better idea of the seriousness of the episodes."

She straightened and gazed straight into his eyes. Adam's mouth went dry. Yes, he did resemble a seventh grader.

"I say things I don't mean, especially when I'm upset," she said.

Rachel had the market on loveliness. Adam couldn't keep his attention off her face. "We're all guilty of saying things we regret later."

"But some of us have a hard time apologizing." Her smile faded, and in its place was a near frown. "I'm sorry about this afternoon."

"Me too," he managed.

"I think hurt and pride took over," she said.

"Understandable."

"I need a good lawyer and a friend." Rachel's shoulders lifted and eased back down. "Are you interested?"

"Yes—in both. Shall we scrap this afternoon and start again with me walking you home from work?"

Rachel toyed with the soiled cloth in her hand. "I'd like that very much."

"Rachel," Joan called from the kitchen doorway. "I'd like to close in ten minutes. Are you nearly finished?"

"Yes, Ma'am."

"Good. Five-thirty in the morning okay? Just found out we're going to be shorthanded."

"Fine," Rachel replied.

Adam admired her commitment. If he stopped to think

about it, Rachel valued all of her responsibilities. He questioned how her mother failed to see this fine attribute. Thelma Myers obviously dwelled too much in the past.

Within fifteen minutes, Adam covered Rachel's shoulders with his jacket, and the two stepped out into the chilly night air.

"Thank you. It's a bit cold," she said.

"You're welcome." Odd, for an attorney, he couldn't think of a single thing to say. The thought of what this meant slammed into his face once again. *Remember your client-lawyer relationship.*

"I forgot to ask you today about Bud," she said. "Is he keeping his nose clean?"

Adam shrugged. "One minute he's the sweet kid I know and love. In the next, his hormones are raging, and he reminds me of a horror movie."

Rachel laughed. "We've all been there, Adam, some of us more so than others."

"I feel sorry for all parents. This is not fun, but it is a challenge."

"Are you being consistent?"

"I'm trying. I understand my brother let him do whatever he wanted, and I refuse to follow in those footsteps. My job is to let Bud know I love him unconditionally, but there are boundaries and rules for him to follow."

"Sounds like a good plan to me."

Except for a motorcycle whizzing by and the sound of a distant barking dog, silence took over their conversation. They were within a half block of Rachel's apartment.

"I will make an appointment to take the placement test," she finally said. "I've been thinking about the problem, and I've reached some conclusions."

"Which are? If you don't mind."

"When I look back at the situations where I miserably failed at something, pressure seems to rule the moment. Tests are the first thing that comes to mind and the times in school when a teacher called on me. Remember when you had me read and I couldn't comprehend the information? It all points to stress and my lack of self-confidence—just like you said."

A lot more people needed Rachel's ability to see themselves honestly. He was one of them. "You are extremely bright and very perceptive."

"Depends on the situation."

They both laughed.

"I'm glad you're taking the initiative on this. I want to see you at the head of your class. What are you thinking about studying?"

Rachel glanced up at the sky. "Promise me you won't laugh?"

"Promise."

"Two items are of great interest to me, and they are linked. One is psychology. While I was doing my six months for society, I found an interest in the subject. The second one is working with women, perhaps in social services. I've thought about a Christian rescue mission and even a prison ministry." By this time they were in front of the bakery with only the street lights to illuminate her face.

Adam pictured her in either of the roles and doing a fine job. He recalled the way she had spoken to Bud. If that was an indication of her abilities, she'd be perfect. "All I can say is wow. You'd be dynamic."

"Thanks. I'm praying through them. When I have idle time—which isn't often—I dream about helping women who were just like me. I want to tell them about Jesus and have the tools to show them a way out of their circumstances." She shrugged. "When I say circumstances, I mean spiritually, physically, and emotionally." She pressed her fingertips together to form a circle. "All of those things together mean success for the woman who feels beaten and useless."

"You have empathy for those women," Adam said. "By experiencing those things yourself, you could relate much better than a trained professional, who has only sympathy and book knowledge."

"You are great for a woman's ego." She laughed, and the

musical sound made him feel ensnared by the schoolboy syndrome he was trying to avoid.

"I'm a lawyer. We're cut and dry—to the letter of the law."

She looked at the stairway leading to her apartment and slid his jacket from her shoulders. "I need to go inside. Besides, you're freezing."

"I'm fine, but you have to get up early. Do you mind if I stop in for coffee tomorrow morning after I drop Bud off at school?"

She tilted her head. "Why, Adam?"

The darkness concealed the warmth creeping up his neck, and he thanked God for it. "Do I need a reason?"

"I'm curious. Would you spend as much time where I work if I had a job in a. . .lady's clothing boutique, a funeral home, construction site?"

He forced a chuckle.

"I'm serious. Are you checking to make sure I'm really rehabilitated? I mean, if you are, that's okay. I have nothing to hide."

Adam dug his fingers into his palms. He fought hard to keep from reaching for Rachel and pulling her into his arms. "I believe you are, Rachel Morton, a good Christian woman who is living her life for Jesus."

"No doubts about my past?"

He shook his head and jammed his hands into his pockets. "It's so cold out here. I need to go."

He reached out and touched her arm. "No, one minute, please. If my presence at the restaurant makes you uncomfortable, I'll stop. But the reason I'm there is you, Rachel."

Her incredulous stare caused him to release her arm.

"I'm your attorney, and I will continue to represent you to the best of my ability." He stuffed his hands back inside his pockets. "When this is all over, when you have your children, and you're heading into a great future, would you consider pursuing a relationship with me?"

eleven

Rachel opened the restaurant with Joan the following morning. She'd gone to bed as soon as she'd mounted the steps to her apartment the night before, but she hadn't been able to sleep. The conversation with Adam rolled around in her head until she didn't know if she were dreaming or if he'd really said those things. She must have fallen asleep at one point, because in her sleep world, Slade had accused her of being unfaithful with a no-good lawyer.

Would you consider pursuing a relationship with me? A simple request from a man who had stolen her heart.

She filled decanters with decaf and regular coffee and stuffed small baskets with blue-and-yellow cloth gingham napkins for the homemade biscuits and muffins. The tantalizing aroma of fresh-brewed coffee and baking bread caused her stomach to rumble. The sensation betrayed her, since the last thing she wanted at five-thirty in the morning was something to eat.

Again, Adam's words swirled through her head. Rachel remembered how her heart had raced when he spoke them. She *had* seen those emotions in his eyes, but why? If she looked at things realistically, they'd known each other but a few short weeks. Intelligent, logical people didn't behave this way. Lasting relationships took years of good communication bathed in prayer.

"Adam, I don't think you're being honest with yourself," she had responded last night.

"Oh, but I am, and you have no idea how difficult this is for me."

"We are the most unlikely couple in all of Texas. Look at our backgrounds. What would the society page of the *Brenham Banner Press* say? 'Attorney Adam Raeburn is now dating his

84

client, Rachel Morton, a former drug addict and inmate.'"

"I don't care what anyone says." Adam's frustrated tone touched her. "I live for God and His purpose, not for town gossip."

"I care about what is said." *I care about you too much to subject you to my problems permanently.* Rachel started for the creaky wooden stairs, then she turned back around to face him. She needed to push him away. "Are you sure you haven't fabricated these feelings because you feel sorry for me?"

"No!"

Rachel jumped. "All I'm asking is for you to think about it. This is your future at stake—yours and Bud's."

"Are you telling me that you don't have any feelings for me whatsoever?" Adam asked.

Rachel was caught one more time in the pendulum between a lie and the truth. Already she ached because of the way she'd thrown his emotions back into his face. Whirling around, she hurried up the stairs out of the cold and away from Adam's arms.

In the morning shadows of near dawn, the time of day when hope reigned over despair, she regretted every word spoken to Adam. She felt worse than last night. Foremost in her thoughts was her relationship with Jesus Christ. Second came her relationship to others—her precious children, her parents, dear friends, and Adam. By placing herself last, she gave up selfishness. Too many years had passed where self-centeredness ruled her life. No more. She'd begun a professional relationship with Adam to obtain custody of Autumn, Summer, and Rocky. This must continue to be her focus.

During her break between breakfast and lunch, she'd call Mom to check on Rocky. Rachel thought about apologizing, but for what? Mom had lashed out at her, not the other way around. Even so, she knew her mother, and the blame always rested on Rachel's shoulders.

A couple of years ago, Mom had had a heart attack. The near-death experience softened her for a long time, but after Rachel returned from prison, the old bitterness and sarcasm returned.

With a deep sigh, Rachel watched a familiar couple sit in her area. Glancing at the clock, she saw it read after seven. Where was Adam? He never missed his morning coffee. Then again, why should he come in today or any other time? She'd run him off.

※

Four days had passed since Adam last spoke to Rachel. He worked on her case, gathered credible witnesses, prayed for her, and conducted business as usual. He wanted to call her, but unless he had a professional question, it looked pointless. In short, he wore "bad attitude" like a banner across his forehead.

"I brought you a donut," Anna said as he began another day. "Thought it might sweeten your disposition."

He scowled. "If you have something to say, just spit it out."

"All right. You've been in a rotten mood all week. You're crabby, and you've locked yourself behind that door like a hermit."

"I've got an agenda on my mind."

"Imagine that."

He narrowed his gaze but said nothing.

"Is the problem Bud or Rachel?"

Fury wound its way through his body. Lack of sleep didn't help. "What makes you think the problem is personal?"

Anna set the white pastry bag on his desk. "At least you admit there's a problem. And since I know your cases and clients are in good order, Bud or Rachel must be the center of your enormous heart full of love and good will."

Adam massaged his neck. Anna had given him a heavy dose of the truth. "I'm sorry. I didn't know I was so. . .insensitive."

"Do you want to talk?" She pulled one of the chairs closer to his desk.

"No point. I understand the situation perfectly."

"Then the problem is Rachel. You would handle Bud in a different way."

He leaned back in his chair. Talking about Rachel would not help a bit.

"Is her case not going well?" Anna asked.

Adam shook his head. "Her defense is going better than I expected. I believe the judge will award her custody."

She removed the chocolate buttermilk donut from the bag and placed it on a napkin beside his coffee. "When you want a listening ear, I'm on the other side of the door."

Adam chuckled. "I appreciate it. And I'll try not to be such a grouch."

The phone rang, and he snatched it up before she pried any additional information from him. Anna smiled and slipped from the room.

"Adam Raeburn here."

"Mr. Raeburn, this is Mrs. Warren, the vice principal at the junior high. We have an issue here with Bud."

Oh, great. "What's the problem?"

"He got into a fight during PE. Bud has a bloody nose and the other boy has a black eye. Considering the previous problem with alcohol, we believe he is a threat to the other students."

Adam closed his eyes, wishing the nightmarish phone call to vanish.

"Mr. Raeburn, we need for you to pick up your nephew."

"I'd like to talk to you a few minutes privately before I remove him," Adam said. "In order for me to speak effectively to him about his behavior, I need the particulars on the incident."

"I understand. However, you can talk all you want. Nothing will change my mind. How quickly can you be here?"

Adam glanced at his appointments. "I am on my way. Mrs. Warren, I'm sure there is an explanation for today's incident. Bud's involvement in counseling has indicated a genuine desire to improve his social skills. We've talked about his interests and listed goals—all of which list his education as a priority. Every night he has me check his homework, and we talk about what happened at school that day."

"Sounds like progress, but the fight today is an indication of hostility. We simply can't ignore this. As his legal guardian, you must assume responsibility for his actions."

"I'm fully aware of my position as his legal guardian."

"Pent-up anger could be part of the problem in view of his abandonment. We'll talk more when you get here."

"Thank you." Adam hung up the phone. Could things get any worse? He grabbed his keys and cell phone. Taking a bite of his donut, he called to Anna. "I've got to pick up Bud at school."

She stood in the doorway with a stack of files. "Is he ill?"

He caught her gaze. "He probably wishes he'd contracted an incurable disease. My nephew got himself into a fight."

She shuddered. "I'd better pray for him. In the mood you've been in, he's going to need it."

A short while later, Adam sat in Mrs. Warren's small office. She had more piles of papers on her desk than he did. All the butterflies and daisies decorating her workspace made him feel like he was in a ladies' tearoom. She explained the fight in PE.

"What you're saying is a student called Bud a name, then made reference to his parents?" Adam asked.

Mrs. Warren, a no-nonsense woman in her late forties, nodded her head. "Yes. The other boy admitted to the fact. Bud threw the first punch."

"And what is the school's recourse for this type of behavior?" Adam asked.

"I have no choice but to recommend him to the district's alternative learning facility. I plan to make arrangements tomorrow."

Adam groaned. "Where he'll learn more bad habits from kids who can't behave themselves in the regular school system?"

Mrs. Warren took a deep breath. "I'm sorry you feel that way. We have considerable success in this program."

"Do I have any other options?" This wasn't her fault; she had rules and guidelines to follow.

"You might consider home school or a private school." She handed him a sheet of paper with the phone numbers of two private schools. "Both of these are excellent facilities."

Adam folded the paper and stuck it in his jacket pocket. "Thank you for your time, Mrs. Warren. I'd like to take Bud now."

In an outer office, Bud sat with an armload of books and papers, obviously the contents of his locker. His eyes read of sadness and a twinge of fear.

"I did it this time." He avoided Adam's stare.

"I'll say you did." Adam took the majority of his things, and they pushed through the glass doors and on to the parking lot. He didn't know what to say without exploding.

"Who was the other kid?" he finally asked.

"Mrs. Warren's son."

❧

Rachel counted four days since she'd seen Adam. Every morning she looked for the familiar dark brown hair and wide grin. She attempted to tell herself this was the best for all involved, but her heart still ached.

To keep every hour filled, she visited the nearby college and arranged for the placement test on Thursday morning of the next week. Once Rachel identified her problem in taking tests was a lack of self-confidence, she began praying for God to release her of those things that did not honor Him. Pastor Johnston talked with her about the test and helped her understand the past problems with her mother could have a significant impact on her self-confidence.

Another matter plagued Rachel and that lay in making another visit appointment. She had thirty minutes before time to leave for work. Breathing a prayer for courage, she grabbed the phone and called the boutique. Mom answered on the third ring.

"Hi, Mom. How are you?"

A moment of silence filled Rachel with dread.

"I'm well, thank you." An iceberg could not have been colder.

"Are the kids okay?"

"Yes. Summer is now being tutored, and already we've seen improvement in her reading."

"Please tell her I'm proud of her."

"Let's not be hasty with praise until her grades improve," Mom said. "I wouldn't want her thinking she is a better student than she really is."

Rachel nibbled at her tongue to keep from saying exactly what she thought of her mother's tactics. "I was thinking more of building her self-confidence."

"And why did you call?" her mother asked. "I have customers in the store."

"I'd like to set up another time to visit my kids."

"Sunday seems to work fine."

"Perfect. I'd like to sit with you in church," Rachel said.

"The pew isn't long enough. I have to go now."

Rachel swallowed hard. "Mom, I've filed for custody."

"So, I've heard. You don't have a chance. You know that."

"I'll wait and see what the judge says. Mom, are you not feeling well?"

"Rachel, I'm busy."

The phone clicked in her ear, and Rachel decided to visit the boutique in the morning before work. The last time her mother became this harsh, she had a heart attack.

Lord, watch over my mom. She's a bit crusty on the outside, but I know it's because of her love and concern for the children. Please help me to love her as You do.

Tugging on her sweater, Rachel grabbed her apartment keys. The phone rang just as she turned the knob on the door. Thinking it might be her mother, she dashed back to the phone.

"Rachel?" a male voice asked.

"Yes."

"This is an old friend of Slade's. How ya doing?"

Rachel shivered. A haze of a million ugly memories clouded her mind. "Who is this? What do you want?"

"No need to get testy, Rach. Me and Slade had some good times together. I'd like to see you."

"No, thank you. Slade is dead, and I've gone on with my life."

"So you're Miss Clean now?"

Rachel sucked in a breath. "Don't ever call me again."

She hung up the phone and clasped her arms around her shoulders. Once more she started for the door. The phone rang again, but she dared not answer it. For once she was thankful for not owning an answering machine. Standing in the doorway, she waited until it stopped ringing. A moment later, the phone began again. This time she left her apartment, making sure to lock it securely behind her.

Fear seized her senses. She remembered the times Slade had beaten her and then bragged to his friends afterward. All those times he got high and spent all their money, until she finally gave in and did the same. The pattern continued until she had to get away. Rachel knew life meant more than the drug world, and she had three children whom she loved with all her heart. Once she left Slade, she vowed to never sink to those depths again. The thought of a face-to-face meeting with one of those guys made her skin crawl. How did he find her? She and Slade had lived in San Antonio back then. How did the man get her phone number? Rachel tried to pray, but she didn't know what to ask. Protection? Guidance?

Her attention focused on the restaurant mere footsteps away. She quickened her pace. A gust of February wind caught under her sweater and chilled her. When at last she inhaled the familiar smells and heard the lively sounds of laughter and easy conversation, Rachel breathed evenly. If the man ever phoned again, she'd have her number changed.

Tying on her apron, Rachel's gaze swept across the restaurant. There sat Adam and Bud in her section with no drinks or food.

twelve

Adam thought Rachel looked pale. *She must be working every minute of the day.* When she walked their way, he grinned in hopes of cheering her, and she offered a faint smile in return. He'd intended to avoid this restaurant and keep his meetings with Rachel at the office, but Bud wanted to come for an early dinner since both of them had skipped lunch. Today had been at the bottom of the list of days he'd want to repeat. It couldn't end soon enough.

"Hi. How are you guys doing?" she asked.

"Good," Bud said. The boy seemed to be relieved that he no longer had a school to attend. His good nature struck a sour note in Adam. When she turned to him for a response to her question, he faked a "great."

"Iced tea and a Coke?" she asked.

They nodded, and she disappeared.

"Looks like you and Rachel are still having problems," Bud said.

"You know, Sport, I'm not in the mood to discuss Rachel. You and I have a problem to solve, and it's no more settled than it was this morning when I carted you out of school."

Bud raked his fingers through his hair. "I know I disappointed you, but the guy made me real mad. He said horrible things about my parents." He shrugged. "They were true, but he didn't have to say it."

"Fighting doesn't solve anything."

"Made me feel real good." Bud glanced up at his uncle. "I'm not sad about the school thing. I've been thinking, and maybe I need to start all over again like Rachel did."

"Tell me more." Adam mentally braced himself for whatever Bud suggested. At that moment, Rachel returned with

92

their drinks. She scribbled down their food orders and slipped back into the kitchen.

"Teachers and the other kids expect me to get into trouble, so I do. Not always on purpose. It just sorta happens." Bud took a drink of his Coke. "I don't want to ever go back to my dad's again. I want to stay with you. I see what you're doing as a lawyer—helping people, going to church, and stuff. I want to be like you."

If the two hadn't been in a public place, Adam would have shed a few tears. In the next breath, he realized the remorse could be a ploy. "Do you have any ideas?"

Bud hesitated before he answered, as though he groped for the right words. "One of the schools listed on Mrs. Warren's paper is a Christian school. If they would accept me, I'd like to go there. I don't know about the cost, and you're already taking care of me."

"The tuition is not your concern. If you honestly believe a fresh start in a Christian environment is the best solution, and you are willing to try as hard as you can, I'll do my best to get you in."

"I promise, Uncle Adam."

"Your chances are dwindling, Sport. This is serious business."

"You might not believe this, but I have been listening in church and Sunday school, but I'm confused about what Pastor Johnston means by a personal relationship with Jesus. It doesn't seem real."

"We can talk about it right now." Adam wrapped his arm around the boy's shoulders, not caring if Bud believed he was too old for affection. "I love you, Bud, and I want God's best for you. Life is filled with tough things—like walking away from fights—but the Bible says all things are possible for those who love God and His ways."

"I'm beginning to understand, but I'd rather wait until we get back home from dinner. I've made some notes over the past few days with questions and stuff, and they are in my room. Besides, I'd rather we talk private."

"We can get carry-out."

Bud shook his head. "This is fine. Uncle Adam, I don't want to ever end up like Dad and Mom."

"I guess now is as good a time as any to tell you this. Your dad and mom have signed over permanent custody to me. What I want you to know are their comments to me about it."

"I can only imagine." Bud blinked a few tears, then reached for his drink.

"Your mother cried. She said she loved you but she didn't know how to be a good mom. Your dad said he loved you enough to realize the best place for you was with me. I've never been a dad, and I'm scared to death, but it looks like you're stuck with me."

Bud stared ahead. "Sounds a lot like the problems Rachel's having. She loves her kids, but the best place for them is with someone else." Before Adam could pray through a reply, the boy continued. "Except Rachel is doing all the good stuff to get her kids back."

When Rachel brought their food, Adam attempted to act normally, whatever that might be. "Would you call Anna and set up an appointment?" he asked.

"I can. Are their new developments?" Rachel wrung her hands, then smoothed her apron.

"I wanted to speak with you about witnesses, housing plans. I have a list."

"Okay. I'll call in the morning on my break."

"Is Thursday the only day you can see me?"

She tilted her head. "Yes, although next Thursday I take my placement test." She took a deep breath. "I could squeeze in an hour on Monday morning before work."

"Sounds good to me, but check with Anna." Adam hated the sound of his robot-like voice—programmed to only transmit information.

❧

The weekend slipped by with Mom canceling Sunday's visit due to not feeling well. Suspicion continued to needle at

Rachel about her mother's health. Mom could fake headaches to have her own way, but Rachel remembered how ill-tempered she became prior to her previous heart attack.

How wonderful if Rachel and her mother had a better relationship. Mom served Jesus and loved Him, but she had a difficult time forgiving Rachel for the past. *How many times must I tell her I'm sorry?* The key issue revolved around trust. Rachel understood she must earn credibility, but how long before her mother's doubts disappeared?

Monday morning, Rachel finished ironing her uniform and slipped it over her head. She'd taken a little longer with her hair and makeup this morning, scolding herself the entire time. Looking her best for a man she intended to deter made no sense at all.

She set the hot iron by the sink and put the ironing board into her overstuffed closet. Adam needed definite housing arrangements for her and the children. The government-funded apartments had placed her name on a waiting list some time ago, and she'd check on her status with them this morning. Providing for Autumn, Summer, and Rocky would be a tight squeeze both financially and timewise. She'd talked to Joan about her hours, and she assured Rachel they'd work out a schedule giving her a few nights off. She didn't want the court date to find her unprepared.

Rachel snapped off the light in her tiny bathroom, then dropped her keys into her purse. The phone rang. Thinking it could be Adam's office, she answered it.

"Well, good morning, Rachel. This is Jimmy."

Rachel sensed her fingertips tingling. She now recognized the source of the voice from this and the previous call. Her mind flooded with memories of a face more evil than any other person she'd known. "I asked you not to call anymore."

"I don't take orders from anyone." Jimmy's ominous voice sent a path of dread and panic up her spine.

"What do you want?"

"To meet with you, like I said before."

"Impossible, so give it up," Rachel said.

Jimmy chuckled. "Slade had something of mine, and I want it back."

"I have nothing of his."

"You're a liar."

Rachel's face grew warm, and she trembled. "Look, Jimmy, I'm not lying to you; neither do I know what you're looking for or where it is."

"I have ways of persuading people to my way of thinking."

"This conversation is over." Replacing the phone, she took a deep breath in an effort to slow her pounding heart.

The phone rang again, but she snatched up her purse and rushed outside. Her comfortable shoes made a little *whish* sound as she descended each step. She scanned the small parking lot behind the building and saw no one standing nearby. For the next several seconds, she studied the area around her. When she felt certain no one lurked about, she hurried to her car. All the way to Adam's office, she kept taking quick glances in her rearview mirror. A mental image of a dirty, greasy man formed in her mind. Her stomach churned. He'd done time with Slade; he'd been involved not only in drugs, but also in the robbery of a convenience store. Slade stated once that Jimmy was not a man to mess with. Jimmy had murdered and gotten away with it—more than once.

Anna greeted her warmly at Adam's office for her morning appointment. "Don't you ever eat?" she asked. "You remind me of a fence post."

Rachel desperately needed a diversion from her thoughts. "I've always been thin, and so are you. Lucky, huh?"

"You are pale, more like a ghost, and you look anemic."

Rachel pretended shock. "I must have forgotten my blush." At that moment Adam opened the door. He looked perfect— his suit, every hair in place, even the soft tones of his voice.

"I thought I heard voices. Good to see you, Rachel. Come on in."

She followed, and he closed the door. She must find some

level of confidence around Adam. His keen perception was bound to pick up on her scattered emotions.

Once seated, she observed him leafing through her file. "I phoned the government housing apartments this morning to see about availability. They will have an apartment for me in mid-April. I'm working out a work schedule with Joan, and I'm hoping to take one class this summer."

"Excellent." His professional tone pierced through her heart. Isn't this what she wanted?

"You mentioned witnesses. How many do you need other than my parole officer, Joan, and Pastor Johnston?"

"Possibly your Sunday school teacher. Have you looked any further into daycare or baby-sitting for the children while you're working?"

She nodded. "I interviewed two facilities that are also government subsidized, and I've made a decision. The idea of allowing the government to take care of me until I am established makes me feel more like a charity case, but I'm hoping it's short-lived. Also, I talked to an older lady at church who is willing to watch the children a few evenings while I work the dinner hour."

"Are things any better with your mother?"

She pressed her lips together. "Not really. I'm wondering if she is having heart problems again. After her first heart attack, she made a complete turnaround—we got along great, and she treated everyone with respect. Dad told me she hasn't been taking her medicine. I have no clue why—probably just stubborn. I do know she gives the children her undivided attention and still works four to five days a week at her dress boutique."

Adam rubbed his palms. "The lawyer side of me says why bother, but the Christian side says to keep trying and to pray for God to speak to her."

"I plan to. I stopped into the boutique to see her, but she was too busy with customers. We could be a happy family if she'd let me inside her heart."

"Trouble knows no boundaries, does it?" Adam asked.

When she agreed, he plunged deeper. "Rachel, you were trembling when you came in here. Do I bother you that much?"

She shook her head, and her gaze darted about the room.

"I apologize for speaking too soon about. . .us."

She smiled faintly. "Adam, I didn't mean to be so rude that night, running like a kid afraid of the dark. All I wanted was to show you the foolishness of what you were suggesting. I'm not the woman for you." She glanced out the window behind him. "You're a wonderful man, and you deserve an educated woman who doesn't have an ugly past."

⁓

"I'd rather be the judge of that, or rather God will." He picked up a pencil and toyed with it. He pushed aside the hurt tugging at him. "In any event, is that what's bothering you?"

Her face paled, and he saw something akin to terror.

"Rachel, what is it?"

"There's nothing you can do."

"Try me."

She stood from the chair and then sat back down. "I've received two phone calls from a man who used to do business with Slade. He wants to see me, and both times I've refused. His second call came when I was leaving my apartment. He believes I have something of his, something either Slade stole or kept for him."

"Do you have a name?" Adam remembered Slade's reputation, and a friend of his would have no problem bullying a woman like Rachel.

"Jimmy. No last name, and I can't remember it. Believe me, I've tried. He's worse than Slade."

"How did he find you? I thought you had an unlisted number."

"I do. And when Slade knew him, we lived in San Antonio. I have no idea how he found me, much less located my phone number."

"There are ways. Unfortunately, unless he threatens you or we get a last name for the police, nothing can be done."

"I understand," she said through a raspy voice.

"Would you promise to call me if he does this again?"

"I suppose."

"Promise me."

"All right, I'll call. But he knows I have nothing of Slade's. Bothering me would be a waste of time."

"If he's gone to this much trouble to find you, he's not about to give up easily. Be careful. Guys like this play for keeps."

For several moments, she sat quietly. "One more thing, he said he had ways of persuading me."

Adam clenched his fists. "That's a threat. Do you think you'd recognize a picture of him?"

"I could try."

"For the police, that may be all you need to have him picked up. Let's talk to them."

"Adam, I don't have much time."

"I'll pay you out of my pocket." Her priorities bothered him—a lot. "Look, we'll call Joan along the way and explain you might be a few minutes late. I know you place great importance on your responsibilities, but you won't do your children a bit of good if this character decides to act on his threat."

"You don't give me much choice," she said.

"I'm a determined man, in more ways than one."

thirteen

At the police station, Rachel waited in a chair beside Adam while a detective searched through the computer files for a man named Jimmy who fit the description and background information she'd given him. She sat with her hands neatly folded in her lap. Adam said identifying Jimmy was important, but she had to be at work in thirty minutes.

She felt strange being at a police station without being arrested. Icy fingers of the past clawed at her resolve to stay calm. In her younger years, she refused to say a word until her lawyer arrived. She remembered watching the front door for her parents and being ashamed of her behavior. Unfortunately, she hadn't been ashamed enough to stop.

The longer Rachel sat there and listened to the happenings around her, the more she realized policemen were public servants, not the enemy she had categorized them as in days gone by. The months in jail had given her time to evaluate her preconceived ideas about a lot of things.

"Miss Morton," the detective said, "would you take a look at these mug shots and see if any of them resemble the man you knew as Jimmy?"

Adam reached over to give her hand a squeeze. Rachel should have pulled away, but the touch felt comforting—and safe. Fear had seized her, and although she knew God watched over her, she wondered who was watching Jimmy.

Turning her attention toward the computer screen, Rachel stared into the face of the bearded man she knew to be Jimmy. "That's him." She shivered. His beady eyes frightened her, reminded her of the times he stayed uninvited with her and Slade. If Slade went to any extreme to appease him, then Jimmy must be capable of anything.

"Are you absolutely certain?"

Rachel nodded. "Slade said he'd slit his mother's throat for a dime."

The detective, a fellow in his forties with more hair growing from his ears than his head, nodded. "Jimmy Baldwin. Huntsville released him from prison two weeks ago."

Adam squeezed her hand again. "What do I do now?" she asked.

The detective swung his chair around to face her. "We'll follow up on Baldwin and let him know he's not playing games with us. In the meantime, be careful. Keep your doors locked. Don't go out alone after dark—"

"Sir, I walk home from work at night," she said.

"I'll escort her," Adam said.

"Good. Miss, keep us posted of anything unusual, and we'll contact you as soon as we locate Baldwin."

Rachel left the police station feeling more alarmed than when she'd arrived. When she left Slade, she left his possessions behind. What did he have that belonged to Jimmy? Whatever it was, this dangerous man wanted it back.

She tripped on the curb, and Adam caught her arm. "Easy. The police will catch up with him before the day's over." He took a glimpse at his watch. "And you will be at work on time."

"Thanks. Guess I'm a bit clumsy this morning."

He chuckled, and she appreciated his efforts to calm her unraveling nerves.

"Maybe I need to pass on some of Greg's stress-relieving techniques," he suggested.

"He already has. I'm the one who has problems with tests, remember?"

He held on to her hand and turned her to face him. "Don't try to ace any test where Baldwin is concerned."

Rachel nodded. If she attempted to say a word, she'd dissolve into a puddle.

With the extra time she'd be spending with Adam after work hours, she'd have to fight her emotions around him.

Why did things always seem so hard, so complicated? All she ever wanted was custody of her children. Now, she had to deal with her growing feelings for Adam, consider the possibility of her mother facing another heart attack, Autumn's rejection, taking tests for school, Jimmy Baldwin and his threats, and whatever else came knocking on her door.

"I'm always here to lend a hand if you fall."

"What if I didn't have any problems?" she asked. "What if you were the one who needed help?"

By now they were at the passenger's side of his car. She turned to face him, conscious of him standing inches from her. "If you were bleeding, couldn't walk, who would you want to be Jesus to you?"

"I understand what you're trying to prove, Rachel, but you're wrong. My feelings for you have nothing to do with pity, sympathy, or my ego. This involves a matter of the heart. Don't you think I've talked to God about us?" He unlocked the door, and she stepped aside for him to open it. "And for the record, you are the one I'd want to help me up."

"Thank you." She combed her fingers through her hair. "Adam, I value our friendship, but I refuse to lead you on or see you hurt."

"I'm a grown man, Rachel. I think I can handle myself."

"Well, Mr. Crusader, I think you need to reevaluate your feelings."

She slid into the seat, and he slammed the door, a little harder than what she thought necessary. When he climbed into the driver's side, she noticed his tightened jaw and the pronounced lines around his eyes just before he slipped on his sunglasses. He reminded her of a turtle, withdrawing into his shell.

"Okay, I'm sorry," she said. "No excuse except I'm stressed to the max, and it's not even ten o'clock." She touched his shoulder, then jerked back her hand.

"Did you get burned?"

"Adam!"

He sighed. "My turn to apologize. I'm behaving like a self-ish, shallow, egotistical male instead of a grown man who is frustrated about this Baldwin character. Let's start all over. I'm getting you to work on time. The police are looking for Baldwin. We will win the custody hearing, God willing."

"Pray." Rachel knew she was on the verge of tears. "Would you please pray for me. . .for anyone who might get in his way? Jimmy gives a whole new dimension to evil. I've seen Slade scared to death just knowing he was heading to our apartment."

He took her hand. Adam was the only man who'd ever touched her with such gentleness. She sensed a strength that she desperately craved, and warmth soared beyond human understanding.

"Heavenly Father, thank You for Your awesome presence in times of trouble. We come to You asking for protection and peace. Rachel has so much on her mind, and she's frightened. Lord, I'm frightened for her. We ask that this man be stopped, and we pray he comes to know You, amen."

Adam's confident tone soothed her trepidation, but she knew it was the power of God working through him. She smiled. Her heart softened at the tender look in his eyes.

Help me, Lord. I do care for this man.

Once at work, Rachel pushed aside the cares and problems weighing on her heart and mind and focused her attention on the task before her. Jesus was the ultimate burden-bearer; He'd see her through these troubles.

❧

En route back to his office, Adam called Brenham's Christian School. The school had been an answer to prayer. During the school searching process, Bud had voiced his opinion about home school, and the idea didn't appeal to him at all. He liked sports involvement and the variety of activities offered at a regu-lar school, although many home-school support groups filled those gaps. Adam would have managed Bud's education and his law practice somehow. Then they visited Brenham's Christian

School, and all the pieces came together. They focused on the total student: mentally, physically, and spiritually.

Earlier in the morning as Bud got ready for his first day, he seemed exceptionally nervous—excited too—because he understood it might be his last chance. Adam believed Bud should have an opportunity to succeed, and he prayed this new school would unlock his future.

The phone rang twice before a woman greeted him. "This is Adam Raeburn. I enrolled my nephew this morning, Bud Raeburn. I'm checking to see if his day is going well."

The receptionist put him through to the principle. A definite kindness radiated through the phone. "One of his teachers just left the office. She thought you might call and wanted to relay a message."

I probably acted like the parent of a kindergarten child on the first day of school. "I'm ready."

She laughed lightly. "He did well for English and math. The students welcomed him, and he seemed to be fitting in. He's in PE at the moment. If you want to call this afternoon, I can give you an updated report."

"What about the teacher who wanted to relay a message?"

"She said he indicated a desire to take an early morning Bible study on Tuesdays and Thursdays. The students meet by the flagpole at seven o'clock. If the weather is bad, they meet in the cafeteria."

"I'll have him there," Adam said. He thanked her and ended the call. He'd made a commitment to give his all to Bud, no matter the cost.

Strange as it seemed, he'd made the same pledge to Rachel.

Inside his office, Anna handed him his messages and reminded him of his appointments. Before he could handle someone else's problem, he contacted the detective at the police station.

"Rachel Morton is my client," he said. "When you pick up Jimmy Baldwin today, I'd appreciate a call."

"Yes, Sir. I've got your card."

Adam felt better in that respect. He'd inform Rachel the moment the police had Baldwin in custody, then the two of them could relax and deal with the hearing. He wondered how one woman could handle so many problems. She'd already been given more than her share, and Adam wanted to solve them all. *Hold on, Fella, that's not your department.*

He needed to heed his own advice: Deal with one problem at a time. Mr. Crusader, she'd called him. Anna had called him the same thing many times in the past. He chuckled despite the seriousness of the day. The truth always had a way of rising to the top.

He read through the pink call-back slips. One of them indicated Archie and Thelma Myers now had an attorney. The attorney asked Adam to call. Adam despised the thought of good people who loved each other fighting it out in court as if love could be bartered in a court of law.

❧

Thursday morning, Rachel arrived at the college for her test fifteen minutes ahead of her scheduled appointment. She'd done nothing but pray for the past two days, and others had enlisted their prayers too. Butterflies danced in her stomach, but she didn't feel sick, which had been her reaction to tests in the past. Adam had helped her prepare, and oddly enough she wanted to take the test and be done with it. If the results indicated she needed English or math pre-college courses, then fine. That's what she'd do.

At the proper time, Rachel opened the test and began. At first, the questions ran into a blur and she had to repeatedly read them. Fright rose like a fog in the early morning.

Help me, Lord. I can't do this without You.

Rachel took a few deep breaths and began again. She reread the question. This time it made sense, and she knew the answer. With praise ringing through the corners of her heart and mind, Rachel went on to the next question. Then the next, and the next.

For the first time in her life, she finished a test in the time allotted and each question had an answer. Handing the booklet to the facilitator, Rachel felt confident—a whole new concept for her—that she'd done her best.

She crawled into her car and phoned Adam. A part of her said her small step toward success didn't warrant bothering him at work, but he had asked her to call.

"I finished the test," she said when he answered. "The whole thing, and I think I did well. I'll know tomorrow."

"Sounds like a reason to celebrate." His voice caused a smile to tug at her lips. "I have an idea."

She settled back in her car and started the engine. "What kind of an idea?"

"Valentine's Day is next week. What about dinner with your lawyer?"

A ripple of excitement bubbled through her. "I'd like it very much, as long as this is purely business."

"Absolutely. Is work a problem?"

She laughed. "Not many people choose country cooking for Valentine's Day. I imagine someone will be willing to trade a breakfast shift for a dinner." She wanted this dinner. They could be friends—friends celebrating a hurdle crossed.

The following day, Friday, was busy at the restaurant. The work force who normally brought their lunches to work chose this day to splurge before the weekend. Ladies enjoyed meeting with friends on Fridays, and the tourist crowd desiring a head start on the various shopping extravaganzas swarmed the streets and restaurants. Tomorrow promised more of the same, but the customers paid the bills and kept Rachel's mind occupied.

Only two more days until her visit. Only a few weeks until the custody trial. She refused to think about the possibility of losing. When her thoughts lingered there, the pain seared her very soul. Adam believed she had a good case, but if the judge ruled otherwise, he'd keep trying the case until they won.

Sweet Adam. How could one man be such a joy and frustration at the same time? Any other lawyer wouldn't have taken her case pro bono or devoted so much time to a single client. He made her feel special, and she liked it.

Early afternoon sped by, and she skipped her break due to the heavy crowds. Tomorrow before work, she planned to stop at the boutique again—take her mother a few flowers and possibly a carrot muffin and decaf coffee. Regular coffee always sent Mom's heart racing.

God loved Mom, and Rachel did too. If the heavenly Father never gave up on His children, she must do the same. Dad had told her that Mom claimed she didn't need her heart medication. That thought struck fear through Rachel, and tomorrow she intended to beg her mother to take care of herself.

Shortly before five, her dad walked into the restaurant. On occasion he stopped in to see her, but never at this time of day. The worried lines on his face alarmed her. He slumped when he walked.

"Can we talk a minute, Honey?" he asked.

She glanced about the crowded dining area.

"I know you're busy, but this is important," he said with no trace of a smile.

She turned to a young man waiting tables beside hers and asked him if he'd relieve her for a few minutes. She ushered Dad toward the food storage room behind the kitchen in hopes they could find privacy.

"What's wrong, Dad? Is it the kids? Mom?" She shivered, but not from the chilly temperatures.

"Autumn had a problem after school today," he said, as though he didn't know where to begin.

"What kind of a problem?" Had her stubborn daughter gotten into an argument with one of her classmates?

"She was waiting for Thelma to pick her up when a man drove by and attempted to lure her inside. He said her grandmother couldn't make it and asked him to drive her home, even said Autumn could use his cell phone inside the car to call. Autumn had never seen the man before and refused. He said she would get into trouble, but she told him she had to have a note from her teacher before getting into the car with someone else. He grabbed for her, and she screamed. The man took off."

Rachel's stomach churned. She grabbed her dad's shoulders. "Is Autumn okay? Did he hurt her? Did the police catch him?"

"Autumn's fine. Shook up a little, but okay. No one got the license plate number, but Autumn gave the police a description of the man. They're looking for him now."

Rachel didn't want to think that Jimmy could be responsible for this, but he was more than capable of such action.

"Dad, I'm afraid I know who tried to nab her." Tears streamed down Rachel's face. She couldn't stop them.

He raised a brow, and she recognized the "you'd better tell me" look creased in his face.

"Earlier this week, I received a call from one of Slade's old buddies. This man used to scare Slade. He's mean, dirty, the epitome of scum. He thinks I have something that belongs to him. I hung up on him. Yesterday morning he called again, and this time he threatened me." She snuffed back the tears. "I had an appointment with Adam Raeburn, so I told him. We went to the police station, where I talked with a detective and picked out his picture from a mug shot. His name is Jimmy Baldwin. He was released from Huntsville about two weeks ago." Breathless, she gasped. "Dad, I have no idea what this man wants. I'd give him my life if I thought he'd leave my precious babies alone."

Dad drew her into his arms. He kissed the top of her head, just like he used to when she was a little girl. "Honey, I hate all of this. It seems the harder you try, the more difficult life is for you. I know you're trusting God, but how much can you take?"

She pulled away from his strong arms. "I don't care about me. I care about my children and you and Mom." She studied his face. "How did Summer escape?"

"The tutor picks her up on Tuesday and Fridays."

"And Mom, is she okay? I planned to stop into the boutique in the morning before work to talk to her about taking her heart medicine. I'm afraid she's going to have another attack."

Dad nodded and drew her back into his arms. "I just came from the hospital. The doctor admitted her when she started having chest pains. I told him she hadn't been taking the medicine. Having her under medical supervision is an answer to prayer."

"Who's going to help with the kids?" Rachel's spirits lifted enough to offer hope about being a mother for only a few days.

"Kristy and Jack Frazier are keeping them."

Rachel knew the couple. They were good people and had befriended her when many thought her faith wasn't real. Jack's niece, Cassidy, had been influential in leading Rachel to the Lord. "But I—"

"Honey, our attorney said that wasn't a good idea." His words, meant to be tender, brought another surge of tears for Rachel.

"What did he think I'd do? Run off with them?"

Dad said nothing.

"Where would I go? Where would I hide? When the judge awards me custody, I plan to stay right here where you and Mom can see them anytime you want. Don't you see my prayer is for all of us to be a family?"

When she stared up at her dad, tears clouded his eyes. "I want the same thing too. I know you've changed. Me and your mom saw the difference before you went to jail, but what's right for Autumn, Summer, and Rocky? At times I think I have the answer, and other times I'm confused."

"That's why we have to let God decide." She reached up with a finger and wiped away a tear on his wrinkled face. "I love you, Dad. We weren't put here on earth as father and daughter to fuss. We're supposed to love each other."

They both cried then. The door opened behind Rachel, and she heard Joan call her name.

"Rachel, what's wrong?"

Taking a deep breath, she faced the dear woman. "A man attempted to kidnap Autumn from school today. The police are looking for him." Later she'd tell Joan the rest of the story. "I'm on my way back to work."

"Nonsense. I didn't step in here to harass you. Have you talked to Autumn?"

"Not yet."

Joan reached inside her apron pocket and handed Rachel the phone. "You call that little girl and tell her she's loved."

"I have the number." Dad pulled out Jack's business card. He raised Arabian horses, and Dad enjoyed visiting his horse farm.

Rachel pressed in the number. Kristy answered, expressed her concern, and gave the phone to Autumn.

"Hi, Sweetheart. Your grandpa is here with me and told me what happened this afternoon after school. I'm so sorry. What a horrible experience for you." Autumn said nothing. Rachel's heart cried out for a response. How she ached to hold her daughter, to hear the sweet sound of "Mommy" from her lips. "I love you, Autumn, and I'm so proud of you for giving the police a description of the man."

Still nothing.

"Are you there, Sweetheart?"

"Yes." The monotone quality of Autumn's voice said fathoms about her desire to avoid talking with her mother. "Grandma is very sick. She's in the hospital. I need to go and help take care of Summer and Rocky."

"I know. Grandpa told me. I'll visit your grandma in the morning."

"She doesn't want to see you. Did you have that man try to take me today? He looked like the kind of man you would like. Why don't you go away and leave us alone? You're not a good mother."

The phone clicked in Rachel's ear.

fourteen

Adam had barely gotten home from work and set his brief-case on the kitchen table when the phone rang. Bud had settled into his homework in front of the TV and had the phone beside him. The boy answered and gave it to Adam.

"Some old guy," Bud mouthed.

Adam took the phone with a mental note to visit with Bud about his first day of school and respect for senior citizens. "Adam Raeburn here."

"Mr. Raeburn, this is Rachel Morton's father, Archie Myers."

"Hello, Mr. Myers. What can I do for you?"

"Rachel's oldest daughter, Autumn, had a problem at school today. A man tried to abduct her. She's okay, just shook up, but I'm concerned about Rachel."

"I'll make sure I see her tonight," Adam said.

"Being her lawyer and all, I thought you should know," Archie said. "She said a man had threatened her a few days ago. She believes he's the same person who used to hang around with Slade. I don't like any of this."

"You're right, and thanks for the call."

Archie hung up, and Adam toyed with the phone in his hand, turning it over and over. How could things get any worse for Rachel? It wouldn't take long for Archie and Thelma's attorney to take today's situation and run with it. The fact Rachel knew the man made her look like a criminal. Add that to her past history, and the custody hearing looked feeble at best.

"What's wrong?" Bud asked.

Adam stared into the boy's face, wondering how he'd feel if someone tried to snatch up Bud. Frankly, he didn't want to go there. "That was Rachel's father. Her oldest daughter was nearly abducted today."

"Sounds like a TV show."

"Unfortunately this is for real. I'm escorting Rachel home from work until the police pick up that guy," Adam said. "Do you want to come along tonight?"

Bud shrugged. "No, I have homework to do and a movie to watch."

"It's Friday night, Sport."

Bud picked up a science book. "I want to get it done. You know, make a good impression on my teachers."

"I'm not too crazy about the idea of you being here alone for all that time."

"I'm twelve years old, Uncle Adam. Have you forgotten what it was like living with my dad?" Bud shook his head.

"Yeah, but you're my kid now."

Bud grinned. "Okay, I'll go and take my book." He hesitated. "Or I might take my headphones and CDs—Christian of course."

"Right." Adam laughed. He hoped Bud's new attitude lasted. "How about pizza for dinner? I have a little work to do."

Adam phoned Greg and asked if a counseling session could be arranged after ten o'clock. "I know it's late, but I'm worried about Rachel."

"I'm concerned too. By all means bring her over to the church. The hour doesn't bother me. I'd be up anyway," he said. "Meet me at the front door of the church."

When Adam and Bud entered the restaurant that night, Rachel looked exhausted, but she offered a smile and a few humorous remarks to Bud.

"I've scheduled an appointment with Greg for tonight." Adam hoped she didn't mind him taking the initiative. "My car is in the parking lot."

Rachel acted relieved. "Thank you. I wondered about phoning him this late. I'm glad you took care of it."

While they drove to the church, Bud filled her in about his new school. Adam hadn't found a moment to tell her about his dismissal from the Brenham public school system.

"Today was your first day?" she asked.

"Yes, and I'm trying very hard to keep my nose clean."

"How nice of your uncle Adam to enroll you in a Christian school. I hope you volunteered to help him on the farm every Saturday for the next twenty or thirty years."

Bud groaned. "I'll probably owe him for the rest of my life, except the farm is a cool place. You'll have to see it sometime."

Adam smiled. His nephew was doing his best to play matchmaker. At least Bud provided Rachel a diversion from the harried day.

"I bet your kids would like it too," Bud said. "The house is awfully big—five bedrooms. I wonder what Uncle Adam and I will do in it all by ourselves?"

"Did you end up bringing a book or your headphones?" Adam asked, wanting to stop the flow of this conversation before Bud proposed to Rachel for him.

"Headphones," Bud said. "I'll sit in the worship center and listen to my music. Take all the time you need."

"Thanks." Adam chuckled. With his nephew around, life would never be dull.

Greg met them at the front door of the church with key in hand. He locked it behind them.

"I am so sorry about you and your little girl," Greg said. "Earlier this evening, I considered coming to the restaurant, but then I figured you would be too busy to talk."

"We were swamped all day, Pastor, but thank you for thinking of me."

"Shall we step into my office?" Greg asked. He smiled at Bud.

"I'm leaving you all to talk," Bud said.

Greg shook Bud's hand. "I hear our Christian junior high has a new student."

Bud peered up at his uncle warily. "Uh, yeah. I started today."

"Wonderful. Let's talk for a few minutes after I'm finished with Rachel."

"Sure."

But he didn't sound enthusiastic. Adam understood the boy's apprehension. He had to tell Greg, his counselor, why he'd enrolled in a new school. Adam had no desire to trade places with a preteen.

"Rachel, do you want to speak with the pastor alone?" Adam asked.

"No," she replied. "I have nothing to hide. Please stay."

Once they were seated in soft, comfortable chairs in Greg's office, the pastor prayed and thanked God for Autumn's safety. "And Lord, give the police wisdom in finding Jimmy Baldwin." He turned his attention to Rachel. "The past two days have been a challenge. Do you want to tell me everything?"

She nodded and told her story, ending with, "After Dad left this afternoon, I finished out my shift, and now I'm here."

"I'd like to think the man decided to leave town rather than face going back to prison," Greg said.

"I hope so," Rachel said. "I'll feel better when he's behind bars."

The quiet peacefulness prevalent in Greg's office's soothed Adam's nerves, and he hoped Rachel felt the same. The warm office colors of deep red and gold had the effect of a blanket on a chilly night. Maybe he was learning something in Greg's stress-management class after all. Silently, he prayed for the same peace to envelop Rachel's senses.

"I want to talk to you a moment about your parents' choice of Kristy and Jack Frazier to keep the children while Thelma is in the hospital," Greg said.

Rachel's lips quivered, and she moistened them. "They are wonderful people. I became good friends with Jack's niece Cassidy during her brief stay in Brenham. What hurts me is I am forbidden to be a baby-sitter for my own children."

"That has to be painful. Is this a court-mandated matter?"

"Yes. My visit is once a week in the company of Mom or Dad or a member of Child Protective Services." She rubbed her neck muscles. "I would not jeopardize the custody hearing by going against court orders, but I can still hope."

"Rachel, I know it's late and you have to work tomorrow," Greg said. "Why don't the three of us pray for God's intervention in your life and in the lives of those you love?"

When the prayer time ended, Greg asked if he could have ten minutes of Bud and Adam's time. Rachel chose to wait in the worship center. Seated in the large room with her stomach in knots and her heart longing for peace, she studied the grand piano. Rachel hadn't played for months, but the sound of music in her head drew her to the keyboard. She sat at the piano and closed her eyes, sensing the Lord calling her into a deeper worship beyond her understanding or her pain. She remembered the pastor stating three things needed to take place for total worship: an attitude of humility, obedience of the heart, and a desire to listen to God's still, quiet voice.

As her fingers moved over the keyboard, melodies of ancient hymns wafted through the worship center. She envisioned Christians of centuries gone by living out their faith in love and devotion, their goals to obey God rather than make meaningless sacrifices. To love Jesus was an honor, to share in His sufferings a privilege. Her songs moved to contemporary praise choruses. Her lips sang the simple words to a God who coveted praise.

"Rachel."

She opened her eyes to see Adam standing midway in the aisle. Somewhat embarrassed at him viewing her private worship, she scooted back the piano bench.

"I'm sorry to interrupt the beautiful music, but you have a phone call."

She startled. "No one knows I'm here. Maybe it's Dad." Dread filled her as she slid from the piano bench. Mom could have gotten worse, or Jimmy Baldwin might have tried another stunt.

"Greg answered the phone, but he didn't ask the name of the caller," Adam said.

Rachel hurried her pace from the worship center into the tiled foyer and on to Pastor Johnston's office. He smiled when he handed her the phone

"This is Rachel."

"Hi, Honey, this is Jimmy. You look real cute in that yeller uniform, a bit skinny for my taste, but you'll do."

She nearly dropped the phone at the sound of the raspy voice. Her hand grasped the corner of the desk to steady herself. "I thought I did a pretty good job imitating your dad's voice. Fooled the preacher there."

"What do you want?" Rachel silently prayed Jimmy would be found soon.

"The money Slade owed me—the money I'm sure you have."

Adam wrapped his arm around her waist. One glance into his face revealed his concern. "Let me talk to him," he whispered, but she shook her head.

"I don't have any money," Rachel said. "If I did, would I be working two and three shifts at a restaurant?" She wanted to scream at him, but through ineffable grace, her voice rang even and controlled.

"Slade took fifty thousand dollars of mine and I intend to get it back. I'd think after today you'd understand I mean business. That oldest girl of yours is pretty, real pretty."

She sank her teeth into her lower lip. "You filthy animal, the police are after you. It's only a matter of time until you're picked up and sent back to where you belong."

"In the meantime, who's protecting your kids? Mommy and Daddy? For that matter, who's playing bodyguard to your lawyer friend?" With those words spit like venom, Jimmy hung up.

Clenching her jaw, Rachel handed the phone back to Pastor Johnston. "It was Jimmy." She gulped. "Says Slade took fifty thousand dollars of his money. He also threatened my children and Adam."

"I'll make sure your kids have police protection," Adam said.

She whirled around to face him. His eyes narrowed, and anger seemed to seep through the pores of his skin. "And what of you? What of Bud? Jimmy will go after all those I care about."

"Call the police," Pastor Johnston said. "Baldwin followed you here and will most likely continue until he's stopped."

Adam contacted the police station and spoke with the detective on duty. "I believe Rachel, her children, and her family need round-the-clock police protection."

Rachel listened, wishing she'd made the call. At least then she could hear the entire conversation.

"Don't tell me you're shorthanded," Adam said. "If something happens to one of them, what's your excuse then?"

Releasing a pent-up breath, Rachel took his hand. Frustration and helplessness etched lines around his eyes.

"I'm sure the press will enjoy your stand," Adam continued.

She studied Bud's face. The rough-and-tough boy of twelve had paled. He'd already seen too much of the ugly side of life. He certainly didn't need anymore.

"Fine, I'll call the chief of police at home tonight and see if he can rectify the matter." Adam paused. "Thank you." A moment later he had a another detective on the line. Adam gave them the phone number for Rachel's parents. "I know we live in a small town where things like this don't normally happen, but I do expect trained professionals to do the job they are equipped for."

"Should I phone Dad before the police do?" Rachel asked. "Remember the kids are at Kristy and Jack's."

"What do you think, Greg?"

"I agree Archie needs to be informed. This might come better from me."

Conscious she still held Adam's hand, Rachel released it. She stole a glimpse of the clock on the pastor's desk. *After eleven.* No matter, Dad needed to know the latest developments. Once more, she listened to a one-sided conversation. Pastor Johnston relayed the information much more calmly than she could have ever done.

After they finished their conversation, Pastor Johnston turned to Rachel. "A call came into your dad while we were talking, most likely the police."

"What a nightmare," she said. "Somebody pinch me so I can wake up."

Hours later, Rachel tossed and turned. A plain-clothes policeman stood outside her apartment door, but the security didn't soothe her raging nerves. The protection eased her troubled mind for this night, but what about tomorrow and the next until they found Jimmy?

Did Slade really take that much cash from Jimmy? For a

moment she pondered what her deceased husband could have done with so much money. In the next breath she discarded the thought. Whether Jimmy had asked for five thousand dollars or fifty, she didn't have it. In any event, that part of her life was in the past. She needed to have faith in the One who ushered in truth.

Once morning came, she dismissed the officer. Rachel intended to check on her mother, then go straight to work. All the way to her car and en route to the hospital, she glanced from side to side and to the rearview mirror. Jimmy was probably sleeping somewhere. Wearing her uniform, she entered her mother's room. Mom lay quietly, hooked to monitors. She looked frail and not the least menacing. At least she wasn't in intensive care.

"Hi, Mom." Rachel showed her a small bouquet of flowers purchased from the gift shop downstairs. "I thought these might brighten your day."

Mom smiled faintly. "Thank you."

"Are the pains gone?"

"Not quite, but certainly not as bad as before." She closed her eyes and sunk her head into the pillow. "I shouldn't have stopped taking my medicine. Of course, hindsight has the best vision, right?"

"Always, Mom." Rachel hoped her presence didn't upset her mother. She planned to stay only a moment and not bring up Jimmy or his call to the church the previous night.

"Why must God zap me to get my attention?" her mother asked. "Why can't He simply tap me on the shoulder or put a piece of Scripture on my mind?"

"I don't have an answer, but I do know the thought of losing you is horrible." She took her mother's hand. "I love you, Mom. Promise me you will take your medication."

Her mother's eyes moistened. "I promise. After all, I have three grandchildren to raise."

Rachel nodded. No words or thoughts formed in her mind—at least none that would not bring pain and strife.

"I love you, Rachel, and I hate this contention between us.

Surely, you can see that your father and I provide the best, most stable home for the children."

"I sincerely appreciate all you have done for them. . .and me."

Her mother squeezed Rachel's hand slightly. "I think we should stop the visits until this man is found, for the children's sake."

The words cut through Rachel. "I agree. Their safety comes first."

"I thought you would. Now, if I could only get you to understand they are better off with Archie and me."

Mom, please.

Her mother turned her head to face Rachel. "I heard you and your lawyer are seeing quite a lot of each other. Do be careful, Dear. Men of his caliber are not interested in a permanent relationship with women who have a troubled past."

"You are probably right." Rachel struggled to keep her tongue in check. Although her thoughts had been similar, she didn't need her mother flinging trash in her face. "I need to get to work, and I don't want to tire you out." She stood and kissed her mother on the forehead.

"Thank you for the little visit and the flowers." Her mother fought to keep her eyes open.

This really exhausted her. "I'll be back to see you tomorrow afternoon before heading into work," Rachel said. "I'm praying for you."

Outside, she scanned the hospital's parking lot for signs of Jimmy. Assured he was nowhere around, Rachel drove on to her apartment, parked in back, and hurried to work.

As usual, her senses alerted to the familiar sights, smells, and sounds of the restaurant. Joan exited from the kitchen and waved with a smile.

"Got a minute?" Joan asked.

"Sure." Rachel snatched up an apron and followed her to a quiet corner in the dinning area.

"Your troublemaker is up to no good again." Joan shook her head. "I received an anonymous phone call from a man today who asked me why I employ drug dealers."

fifteen

Rachel gasped. "Did he identify himself?"

Joan crossed her arms. "He didn't have to. Had to be that Baldwin fellow. What's wrong with our police force? They should have picked him up by now."

"Jimmy's clever. From what I remember, he's dodged the law from coast to coast." Rachel took a deep breath. "Oh, Joan, I'm so sorry."

"He made me mad, that's all. Takes more than a few threats to shake me up."

"He threatened you?"

She shrugged. "When I told him to mind his own business, he asked me if my restaurant had fire insurance."

Rachel massaged her temples. "This nightmare has to end. Did he say anything else?"

"No, I hung up and phoned the police."

Relief flooded her mind. Joan could be quite verbal when challenged. No point in making Jimmy any angrier.

"Would you feel better if I quit?" Rachel asked. "You have enough hassles without having to put up with my troubles."

Joan laughed. "Now that would be a disaster. You're not skipping out on me. I need you. I'll call up the Texas Rangers if I have to, but you, Miss Rachel, are roped and tied to this restaurant."

Rachel laughed too. She had no reason except the temporary comic relief was just what she needed. "All right. I'm going to work."

"Good, and I hope that handsome lawyer of yours comes in because he always puts a smile on your face."

Thankful for a busy Saturday, Rachel kept occupied. She prayed, she watched the door for signs of Adam or the police, and whenever the phone rang, she startled like a deer in headlights.

Late that evening, Adam and Bud arrived exhausted from working at the farm and wanting a to-go order.

"I can escort myself home from work tonight," Rachel said. "You need your rest."

Adam widened his eyes as though he hadn't heard her correctly. "Wrong answer. I'll be here with Bud a little after ten, and I made sure a policeman is posted outside your door again."

During the walk home, Adam positioned himself on one side of her and Bud on the other. Both males looked like walking zombies from a horror show. They needed protection, not her.

"You'll be at church tomorrow?" Adam asked. "But not the same service as your parents?"

"Right, although I doubt if they'll attend with Mom still in the hospital." With Bud hearing every word, she hadn't explained the earlier conversation with her mother. "Due to everything that's going on, I'm not taking my visit."

He nodded. No doubt too tired to answer. When they reached her apartment, a policeman stood ready for duty. She detested this whole thing. Climbing the steps to her door, she heard the phone ring. Rachel hurried inside and snatched it up.

"This is Jimmy."

She slumped into a chair.

"You can breathe a little easier. I'm leaving town. Cops are everywhere. This ain't worth going back to prison."

Once he hung up, she felt numb, wanting to believe him but yet afraid.

"Rachel?"

She glanced at Adam and Bud in the shadows. "Jimmy is leaving town. It's all over, Adam. We can all breathe easier."

⚬

Four days passed, and Jimmy hadn't phoned anyone with his threats. Adam didn't believe he'd left town that easily, but Rachel stated otherwise.

"He had to realize I don't have his money," she said. "Why should he play the bully and risk arrest? Makes perfect sense to me."

"I still want you to be careful," Adam said.

"I will, or rather I am," she said. "Mom and Dad refuse to let the kids out of their sight."

"I'm not beyond believing this could be a ploy," Adam said. "The best point of attack is surprise."

"You've been watching too much TV," she said with a laugh, but Adam saw the concern in her green eyes.

He kept his sight on Bud, although the boy complained that he wasn't a child, neither did he require a baby-sitter. Adam arranged for Bud's transportation after school to the law office and informed his nephew this mode would continue until the police found Jimmy Baldwin. For the nearly two hours until Adam completed the day's work, Bud did his homework and enjoyed a sandwich Anna had waiting for him.

Rachel protested too when Adam and Bud showed up at the restaurant to walk her home. "Bud needs to be in bed for school, and you need your rest." Rachel acted as though her escorts were an interruption, but Adam gave her the same response he had given Bud.

"People are going to talk about us," she said during a phone conversation.

"Good. Maybe a certain young woman I know will take me seriously."

She sighed. "Adam, I have three children and you have Bud. Count them."

He chuckled. "I have, and it's a wonderful idea. Two boys and two girls, and—"

"Adam, are you crazy? Taking on a ready-made family is not easy. Autumn needs counseling so she and I can be mother and daughter again. Bud has scars that will require the same thing, and who knows about Summer and Rocky? All those things will come before you and me. We'd have a dysfunctional family before the ink dried on the marriage certificate."

"I don't know any families who are not dysfunctional in some aspect." The discussion lifted Adam's spirits. Rachel was willing to talk, which was more than they had managed in the past.

"What is there about me that could possibly attract you?" Rachel's quiet voice whispered of emotion. "We've known each other for such a short time."

"You mean why do I care about you?" When she didn't respond, he continued. "I see a wise woman who has a deep capacity for love. I see a beautiful woman with goals and determination."

"Thank you. I am humbled you think so highly of me, but a lasting relationship requires more. Please pray about what you are suggesting."

Adam nearly stated he'd prayed constantly for days. Why wouldn't she believe him? "What about you?" he asked. "You've never said if you have any feelings for me."

Silence greeted him, and he wished Rachel stood before him. If he could read her gaze, then he'd be able to tell her true feelings. Every time he attempted to broach the subject, she turned away. She had taken his hand that night at Greg's office, and for a minute he held hope in her reaching out to him. Adam desperately wanted to learn the truth.

"Rachel, do you or do you not have any feelings for me?"

"Am I on the witness stand?"

He'd angered her, and right now with the approaching custody hearing, they needed to get along. "This is not an interrogation. If you prefer not to answer, then I can accept that, but when the hearing is over, I want an answer."

❧

Valentine's Day came like a menacing cloud rather than a celebration. In the midst of dealing with Jimmy, Rachel learned she'd done well on her tests and scored more than what was needed to begin college classes. With Jimmy gone, her mother's release from the hospital, and passing entrance exams, she should have felt elated, but instead she fretted about the custody hearing and her fragile relationship with Adam. She started to regret her dinner plans with Adam. The idea of spending an entire evening with him settled on her like having her teeth cleaned only to discover she needed a root canal.

At exactly ten-forty-five, a dozen, beautiful roses arranged with delicate baby's breath arrived at the restaurant. The deliveryman announced they were for Rachel and set them beside the wait-staff's computer. Thrilled and bewildered at the same time, Rachel bent to admire the flowers shimmering from little beads of water misted across their petals and to inhale the fragrant scent.

She lifted a small white envelope affixed to a clear, plastic insert emerging from the arrangement. *Rachel Morton*. She'd received flowers on one other occasion in her life, and those were from her dad when she graduated from high school.

"Thank you," she said to the deliveryman, feeling more than a little emotional.

He smiled. "Happy Valentine's Day."

Without touching a single rose, she memorized each bud and petal. The blossoms, some open and some closed, reminded her of God's promises: perfect, sweet, and worth any wait.

Pulling out the card from the envelope, she read the familiar handwriting. *For Rachel, Because I can't resist the most exquisite flowers for a most exquisite woman. Happy Valentine's Day, Adam.*

"Client and attorney, huh?" Joan crossed her arms over her chest. "And dinner tonight too?"

"Shush," Rachel said. "Someone will hear."

Joan leaned over to breathe in one of the beautiful unfolding buds. "Honey, if someone sent me these, I'd be telling the whole world." Lifting her head, she studied Rachel. "Where is he taking you and what are you wearing?"

Rachel smiled despite her misgivings. "I borrowed a little black dress from Kristy Frazier and squeezed out a few dollars for shoes. And I don't know where we're going." She giggled. "Adam is taking Bud to Pastor Johnston's. Bud is furious, wants to come along."

"I'm sure it will be lovely," Joan said. "You should be pampered and spoiled."

Hours later, during dinner at an upscale Italian restaurant,

Adam contributed only polite and uplifting conversation. He looked magnificent in a black sports jacket and cream-colored sweater, but he appeared so uneasy that Rachel finally had to comment.

"Why are you so nervous?" she asked.

"Me?" He replaced his dinner fork and brushed the napkin across his mouth. "The truth is I want tonight to be perfect."

"It is. The best night of my life—ever."

He grinned. "It's been one month today," he said. "Remember, you first came to my office on January fourteenth."

He'd kept track of this? "It seems much longer. I mean—"

"I know what you're saying. Things started happening around your case, Bud, and Jimmy Baldwin."

She nodded. The roses had touched her. The dinner invitation made her feel like a grand lady, but nothing compared to the fluttering in her heart just listening to Adam talk. She could get used to this—for a long time.

"I wonder if the next month will be as eventful," he said. The flickering candle cast a shadowed light across his features.

Slow down, Rachel. You've known Adam one month. She'd known Slade two years before they married, and the relationship cratered. God had no meaning in her past marriage; maybe things could be different with Adam. Maybe God had blessed her over and beyond what she ever dreamed.

❧

Rachel had hoped her parents would change their mind about visiting on Sunday. After all, Jimmy had kept his word and obviously left town. Her mother, however, denied Rachel's request. She insisted her heart would grow worse if Rachel saw the children. All the reminders of Jimmy's near abduction of Autumn would be more than the woman could handle.

It's an excuse. It hurt. Autumn might never warm up to Rachel again unless definite strides were taken. No one knew better than Rachel the consequences of sin, but nothing would be solved by walking away from her children.

Sunday afternoon drifted into Monday, and the week hurried by with Rachel pouring her heart into her work. For the first time in her life, confidence evolved from her closeness with God and the understanding that He had crowned her a princess.

Every day, Adam walked her home from work. Every day her heart betrayed her. Every day the thought of spending the rest of her life with him and their combined children sparked a sense of joy and challenge.

Most of the time, a hopeful outlook surfaced when she considered the custody hearing. She had a plan that covered the present and the future. However, sometimes at night when sleep evaded her senses, she pondered the misery of living without Autumn, Summer, and Rocky. The pain wrenched her heart. Oh, to wrap her arms around their little bodies and kiss their soft cheeks. *Faith.* She must believe with all her might.

Friday morning before heading to work, she called her mother to set up another visit. This time if her mother refused, Rachel would contact Adam.

"I'm glad you're feeling better," Rachel said to her mother after a brief exchange of pleasantries. "I'd like to set up a time to see the kids."

"Why don't you wait until after the hearing?"

"I don't want to wait until then. The courts have given me the right to see them."

"Well, you don't have to get snotty about it."

"I'm not, Mom. I simply want to see my kids." By now, Rachel felt like she was climbing a mud-coated hill. Just when she reached the top, her foot gave way and she slipped back down.

"Sundays right after church are not good for me. I need a nap."

"Can I drive out to the farm and see them while you are resting?"

Her mother cleared her throat. "I suppose your dad could handle things if the children become upset."

I'm their mother. I can manage their moods. "Good. I'll be there on Sunday just before one o'clock."

"Don't bring candy," Mom said.

"I've never brought them sweets during my visits."

"And come by yourself."

"Mom, who would I bring? I'll be there on time, without candy, and alone on Sunday at one o'clock."

Rachel glanced at the clock. She desperately wanted to talk to Adam. Her resolve to keep him at a distance was waning.

I can't lead him on. I'll see him tonight after work. With a deep breath, she downed a tepid cup of coffee and gathered up her things. Stepping out onto the landing, she watched gray storm clouds move across the morning sky. They needed rain, but her mood yearned for a blue sky and warm temperatures.

She closed the door, and a hand sealed her mouth.

"Do not scream. Do not turn around. Do you understand?"

She nodded. The raspy voice: Jimmy. She felt a pointed object at her back.

"I need a down payment on the cash you owe me." He smelled of unwashed bodies, nightmares, and too many scum-infested jails.

Her lips refused to move until the sharp point of something pierced her.

"Did you hear me?"

"Yes. . .I heard you, but I don't have any money."

"I give you twenty-four hours to find it. Don't go telling your fancy lawyer or go to the police." He reached around and showed her a little, pink purse.

Rachel immediately recognized it as Autumn's. Her first name in white iridescent letters sparkled even in the gloomy morning.

"I believe this belongs to your little girl."

"Don't you touch her."

"Keep your voice down or none of your kids or Mommy and Daddy will live until lunchtime. I'm mighty jumpy with this knife back here. Now, I want ten thousand dollars tomorrow morning right here in a plain bag. Understand?"

"Yes. I'll do my best."

"That's not good enough and you know it. You say nothing to anyone. You can't fool me. I know every move you make." He shoved her. "Walk down these stairs and on to your little restaurant. Do not look behind you."

Rachel's knees shook like a blade of grass caught up by a brisk wind. Every step seemed to be her last. Her heart pounded furiously until she wondered if it might burst from her chest.

Her mind raced with what-ifs and hows. She didn't have ten thousand dollars, and she didn't know how to get the money. The old Rachel would have made contacts and sold drugs. The old Rachel might have considered kidnapping her kids and running from Jimmy and everyone else. For a moment her mind dwelled on the possibility of abducting them. She wouldn't be able to run forever, and when the authorities did catch her, she'd be sent back to prison. Shaking her head, she dispelled the thought.

The old Rachel might have gone to her parents, explained Jimmy's demands, and begged them to come up with the money. The old Rachel might have gone to Adam and promised him anything to help her. She abhorred the thoughts of the woman she once was, the despicable person who schemed and manipulated others to obtain those things she wanted.

The new Rachel, the one who gave her life to Jesus, trusted Him to show her what to do. She believed with all her heart that Jimmy could be stopped, and she'd find a way—a way not involving illegal or immoral maneuvers.

Lord, I trust You to guide me through this horrible mess. I pray for the safety of my children, my parents, Adam, and Bud. Shelter me from taking any action that does not honor You.

Clutching the door to the restaurant, she swallowed the bile rising in her throat. She dared not tell anyone about Jimmy's demands until she could think more clearly. She willed herself not to grow pale, be distracted. Evil did not triumph over good.

sixteen

"Who received the box of candy?" Rachel asked in an effort to push the impending danger from her mind. She shifted her shoulder bag.

"Take a look," Joan laughed. "There's a card attached to the box."

Rachel recognized the crooked handwriting and smiled. Inside the tiny envelope, a card read: *We have a date from one to three this afternoon—approved by Miss Joan. Adam*

She gasped. How incredibly sweet.

A hand slipped around her waist. "Don't you dare refuse that man," Joan said.

"Are you sure?" Dare she hope God had given her a diversion?

"By all means. Rachel, you give this restaurant seven days a week. Relax for a few hours and let Adam dote on you."

How could Rachel possibly enjoy those two hours with Adam when she needed to think through how to handle Jimmy?

"Please. For me," Joan said.

Rachel nodded. "Thank you." She bent to stuff her purse inside a low cabinet designated for waitresses' belongings. A little sting assaulted her back where Jimmy had stuck what she believed was a knife.

"Did you fall or something?" Joan asked. "There's a small blood stain on the back of your uniform."

The terror struck Rachel all over again. "I ran into something. Will my apron cover it?"

"Not sure. The blood looks fresh. Let me take a little cold water to it."

Rachel willed her body not to tremble while Joan rubbed a wet cloth over the blood stain.

"It's gone," Joan said with a triumphant air. "Do you need a Band-Aid?"

"Hmm, probably not. Is there a hole?"

"Itty-bitty."

"I'll fix it tonight." Rachel turned around and forced a smile. She had another hole in her heart, an empty spot that cried out for justice and divine intervention.

"You look tired," Joan said with a tilt of her head. "I should be sending you home for a two-hour nap, but those hours with Adam will work magic, I'm sure."

❧

Adam watched the hour inch past noon. Like a lovestruck kid, he had Anna order lunch for two from the deli, complete with a small loaf of French bread, a round portion of Gouda cheese, and a bottle of clear, sparkling grape juice. Although the weather summoned a bit of a chill and gray clouds loomed overhead, joy echoed in his spirit. He'd begun to nurture a special caring for Rachel, and the feeling had burst into full-fledged love.

A few days ago, he'd bought several books on what God said about marriage, blended families, stepparenting, and the different ways to love. When Rachel won the custody hearing, he'd declare his heart. Today he wanted her to see the farmhouse. As his dream neared completion, he no longer cringed with it sitting next door to his friends' Country Charm—a beautiful bed-and-breakfast. Adam's house, a turn-of-the-century home, had obtained a charm of its own. An interior designer helped him with cosmetic suggestions, but the time had come for specific colors, wall coverings, and furniture designs. He'd postponed those decisions until after Rachel's day in court in hopes she'd help choose those decorator things for their new home.

Greg had committed to praying for Rachel and Adam's relationship, but not without reminding Adam of the problems ahead and the importance of a God-centered marriage.

Within the hour, Adam drove Rachel east out of Brenham on Route 290 for the twelve-minute ride to the farm. "The property borders Rick and Paula Davenport's bed-and-breakfast," Adam said. "You know them, I think."

"Oh yes. Wonderful couple. I think I remember your house."

Adam chuckled. "I've done substantial remodeling in the last couple of months, so please don't hit me with any preconceived ideas about the place."

"Well, it has been awhile."

Adam thought Rachel extremely quiet. The candy might have shaken her a little, especially after the flowers on Valentine's Day. He understood his eagerness—like a child who wanted to play all day long and forego a nap. At present, Rachel didn't want to discuss any type of relationship, and he wanted to talk about it from dawn to dusk. He needed to come up with a witty line or two, but his emotions were a bit wired.

"The house is nearly done," he said. "Bud's been a great help on Saturdays. We've stripped hardwood floors, patched walls—all kinds of projects."

"Sounds beautiful. So you and Bud will move here when you're finished?"

He nodded. "I'd like to run a few cattle and horses. Do the gentleman ranching thing." He slid a glance in her direction. "I brought a little picnic lunch for us." At that moment, raindrops began to splatter on the windshield. "Guess we'll eat inside."

She laughed a little, but he sensed her preoccupation.

"You don't have to worry. I'm not going to kiss you or promise you the moon and stars if you'll be my sweetheart."

"You're not? I'd already made my list of what I wanted."

"Oh, all right. Make sure you keep a copy for your files, and I'll see what I can do."

His pulse quickened as they neared the farmhouse. The outside had undergone a grand renovation—new paint and roof—but the interior improvements were what he really wanted her to see.

"This is certainly not the property I remembered." Rachel craned her neck. "Wow, Adam. I can only imagine what you've done to the inside."

"I'm rather proud of it," he said. "Working with my hands relieves a lot of frustration and stress."

"Pastor Johnston's class must be working."

He smiled. "I started the project long before that, which makes me feel like I was doing something right."

They pulled into the stone driveway, and Rachel got out of the car before Adam turned off the engine. She paused for a moment, then slowly mounted the steps of the new porch. In the next instant, she peered through a window like a child scrambling to see a new puppy in a pet store.

"I have a key." He laughed. "I'll give you a tour if you're sweet to me."

"I'll try." She rubbed her palms together. "Now hurry, my break will be over."

Adam held up the bags containing their lunch. "We'll have to eat picnic style."

"After I see your house."

Adam led her through each room, watching the expressions on her face as he introduced the parlor and its brick, wall-length fireplace; the study with original cherry paneling and the added bookcases; an additional parlor transformed into a game room; the new kitchen redone in light oak cabinetry and blue-gray granite countertops; the new oversized bathrooms and massive master bedroom; and the additional four bedrooms upstairs.

"All the wood." She whirled around. "Every room is beautiful. It reminds me of a magazine layout. To think you are going to live here."

Adam moved to her side. "The rooms need to be filled with laughing kids, games, backpacks, and the smell of chocolate chip cookies."

She took a few steps away from him. "Probably so."

Adam had promised himself that he would not pressure her. All the things he wanted to say must be stowed into the "later" file. "Are you ready to eat?" he asked. "I don't have any furniture, but I have a great set of stairs in the kitchen."

"Perfect."

He led her into the kitchen, and they unloaded the bags before sitting on the steps. Adam stole a glimpse of Rachel picking at her lunch. Her hands shook. Several times she clenched her fists, no doubt in an effort to control her nervousness. A matter definitely nibbled at her mind, more so than when she first came to see him at his office weeks ago.

"Would you like another slice of cheese?" he asked. The grape juice, fresh bread, smoked turkey, and cheese sat on the kitchen counter.

"I haven't finished this one yet." Her gaze swept up the staircase to the landing, where a window seat looked out into the rear of the property. "What a perfect place to curl up and read."

Adam agreed. "I could see you doing that very thing."

She studied him oddly, and he wished he could take back his last remark. Brushing the crumbs from his navy blue suit pants, he carefully formed his words. "I'm being pushy."

Rachel's eyes moistened, and she hastily blinked them away. "This will all be over soon."

"Is that the problem? You're worried about the hearing?" Sitting this close, he wanted to draw her into his arms, assure her of the road ahead.

She stood from the wooden steps and placed her Styrofoam cup of grape juice on the counter. "If I could only take back the years, then I'd have a respectable past, a decent job, and my children would not have suffered from my shame." She rubbed her hands across the granite counter and stared up at the floor-to-ceiling cabinets. "Who knows, you and I could have been more than friends."

"We are already more than friends." He studied the pain in her face, not understanding why she fought his desire to love and protect her.

"Are we, Adam? I've tried not to lead you on, although I do fear your infatuation with me is linked with your crusader instincts."

Across the room, he caught a brief glimpse of the feelings she fought so hard to conceal. "You are not the first single woman I've represented and grown to admire. You are not the first woman I've met who has experienced regret in her life, but you are the first woman who I have grown to care about."

She covered her mouth. "Oh, Adam, you don't know what you're saying."

He laid his food aside and rose to walk toward her. "What must I do to convince you I'm serious? Why would I bring you out here on this rainy day but for you to see the home I want you and your children to share with me and Bud? At times I've wondered if my nephew was the issue here. Other times I assume you have no feelings for me. Tell me what it is, because not knowing the reason is driving me crazy."

Rachel shook her head. "The question has never been you. In all my dreams, I have not imagined a man as fine as you wanting me and my children. I don't feel good enough. . . worthy to be linked with you. Bud will be fine. He's on the right path." She took a deep breath. "And I'm afraid."

Not able to resist the urge any longer, Adam reached to pull her into his arms. She stiffened, then relaxed against his chest. He stroked her dark hair, silky soft and smelling of fresh raspberries. He heard her quiet sobs intermingled with the sound of rain pelting against the roof.

"I don't see how you and I can ever be together," she said.

"Why? I might not know a lot about parenting, but I'm willing to learn."

She nodded and offered a smile. "What about Jimmy? What if he returned and threatened the children, Bud included, my parents, you, me?"

A knot tightened in his chest at the thought. "We'd deal with it. I'm the crusader, remember? And I have faith in the police department and the laws of this country to put away psychos like him. More so, I trust in God's provision."

Rachel lifted tear-stained cheeks. "They haven't caught

Jimmy yet." She wiped away the dampness from beneath her eyes. "You are no match for a madman who cares only about himself."

"Is Jimmy the only reason stopping you from loving me?"

She inhaled deeply and stepped back from his embrace. "Is he not enough?"

"Love has no boundaries or limits," Adam said.

"Love is selfless." Her soft voice rang sweet. "You know those values. I can't be selfish and admit feelings for you when you and the ones I love could be harmed." With those final words, she attended to placing the remains of their lunch in the bags. "I should get back to work, now. Thank you for showing me your house." She glanced up and smiled. "It is beautiful."

≈

Rachel wrestled the remainder of the afternoon and evening with thoughts and ideas of what to do about the safety of her loved ones. At one point, she considered leaving Brenham right after work. A few moments later, she discarded the idea. Jimmy would follow through with his plans whether she left town or not.

When echoes of Jimmy's threats roared through her mind, she attempted to focus on God. With fears racing through her, how could the Creator of the universe direct her? As time slipped by, her thoughts became a whirlpool of trusting God and the terror of Jimmy not having the money in the morning. At ten o'clock he'd accosted her outside her apartment door. Twenty-four hours he'd given her to find the money. At ten o'clock that night, Rachel had no plan or hope, only a fervent plea for deliverance.

She'd found it difficult to concentrate on Adam and Bud's conversation when they walked her home. When Adam asked if she were ill, Rachel responded with a yes. Her heart ached for those she cherished.

With a continual prayer on her lips, she lay in bed and remembered her precious children—their infancy, first steps, first words, their uniqueness. From those memories, she recaptured the moments with her parents. They'd loved and sacrificed for her even when she didn't deserve it. She owed them the same.

At four in the morning, Rachel rose from the bed and without the aid of lights dressed in jeans and a sweatshirt. Tying the shoelaces to her tennis shoes, she prayed she could slip from her apartment undetected. The only choice was through the front door. If Jimmy did see her, she prayed she could get to her car before he grabbed her.

Rachel picked up the phone and dialed Adam's home number. She couldn't remember his cell number, and she dared not risk turning on the light to find the number in her purse. The phone rang once, twice, three times, then the answering machine took over. She kept repeating *Jesus help me* all the while the message conveyed how important her call was and to please leave a number.

"Adam," she whispered, "it's a little after four. Jimmy's back. He contacted me yesterday morning and demanded money. He's threatened all of you, and he's watching my apartment, but I'm going to try to sneak out and get to my parents. I have to warn them before he realizes I'm gone. Please call the police."

She laid the phone back in its place and stepped to the door. Pushing aside her terror, she eased it open. Not one more person would ever suffer for her again.

seventeen

Rachel crept down the steps of her apartment. She scrutinized every shadow and movement around her, certain Jimmy would emerge. His evil face stayed fixed in her mind; the prick of his knife blade fresh in her nightmares. If he used the knife to emphasize a point, what atrocities might he inflict on those she loved?

At the bottom of the steps, she feared her heart might pound until her life ceased to exist. Was this how Mom felt when she had her heart attack? Moving ahead, willing her legs to obey her thoughts, Rachel focused on her car parked behind the metal steps of her apartment. She had her key ready, and for once she was grateful for an unsecured older model that upon being unlocked didn't send a loud *chirp* to anyone nearby.

The trek seemed to take forever. Standing beside the car she'd nicknamed the "boat," she fumbled with the key and dropped it. Unbidden tears threatened to flow, but she swallowed them and bent to feel around for the keys. When her fingers touched the metal, she wrapped her hand around them. Rising to her feet, she prayed for God's help to insert the key into the door lock, because she knew she couldn't on her own. Rachel knew God didn't help those who helped themselves, but He did help those who admitted they could do nothing without Him.

With the click of the door handle, Rachel jumped. She had to calm down. Pulling the door open and listening to the squeak of antiquity, she slid onto the seat, shut the door, and locked it. Again she dropped the keys, this time on the floorboard. She breathed so heavily that she feared someone else was in the car with her. Retrieving the keys, she started the engine and slowly backed out of the parking spot. If only she had a cell phone, then she'd be assured Adam had received her message.

She hoped he understood her need to warn her parents and be there in case Jimmy already had them in his clutches. Rachel knew the lingo and could make promises or do whatever he wanted to ensure the safety of her family. All the way out Route 105 to her parents' farm, a mere fifteen minutes that seemed to take forever, her gaze repeatedly flew to the rearview mirror. No one followed. She was alone.

"Lord, I'm scared," she said. "I'm worried about my children and my parents. Keep them safe."

Her thoughts refused to stay fixed on things of the Lord. Instead they flitted from one terror-filled creation to another. Why couldn't her attention stay rooted on the things of the Lord? It showed distrust, when in actuality, she grasped on to the invisible hand of the only One who knew her plight.

Finally, the outline of Dad's barns loomed in the distance. She'd made it. Now to wake them and wait for the police. Rachel realized she should have gone to the police yesterday and told Adam about Jimmy's threat, but terror had seized her logic. While the police guarded her children, Jimmy could attack one of her parents or Adam or Bud. It took contemplating and praying through the situation until nearly two-thirty this morning for her to see God held her loved ones in the palm of His hand. She must trust and contact those who were trained to take care of such matters. But when it came to her children, she had to be there until the police arrived.

Pulling into the graveled driveway, the stones rustled and seemingly crushed beneath her tires. Dad's chocolate lab barked several times and trotted to the car. A friendly face, even that of a dog, helped release the tension. She turned off the engine and opened the car door.

"Hey, Brown Dog," she said, patting the dog's head. "Thanks for keeping the night vigil. Let's see who we can get out of bed."

"And thank you, Rachel." Jimmy stuck the cold barrel of a gun to the back of her neck. "You saved me a trip. I hope you have the money, 'cause if you don't, I'm going to have a little fun."

The evil creature had been in the backseat all along.

❧

Adam woke to Bud shaking him. "Uncle Adam, wake up. Rachel left a message on the answering machine." He stared into the darkness, trying to remember a strange dream, or had Bud really wakened him?

"Uncle Adam."

He peered up in the shadows to see the outline of Bud's face. "Hey, Bud. What's wrong? You sick?"

"No, nothing like that. I went to the kitchen for a drink and saw the light flash on the answering machine. Anyway, it's from Rachel."

Adam threw off the blanket. "I wonder why she didn't call my cell?"

"You'd better listen to this."

Hurrying to the answering machine on the kitchen counter, Adam pressed the PLAY button and listened to the message. His anxiety about Jimmy had been right on track. His gaze flew to the clock on the microwave: 5:45. *Over an hour ago.* No wonder Rachel acted strangely yesterday. He'd been so absorbed in himself and persuading her to think about a permanent relationship that he didn't note her turmoil. Snatching up the phone, he punched 911.

If Jimmy followed her, it might be too late.

"Get dressed, Bud," Adam said. "Now."

"Are we going to help Rachel?" he asked over his shoulder while racing down the hall.

"I am. You're going to the police station." Adam hurried to his own room for clothes, his wallet, keys, and cell phone.

"But I know how to fight," Bud said. A drawer opened and shut.

"No way." Adam reached for his closet door and the light

simultaneously. He pulled out jeans and yanked on a long-sleeved shirt, sending the hanger to the floor. "And don't argue." Latching on to his boots that held a pair of soiled socks, Adam hollered for Bud. "Let's go. You can finish dressing in the car."

Bud grabbed his headphones on the way out the door.

In the next moment, the two climbed into Adam's two-door sedan and headed toward the police station. Every breath echoed a prayer for Rachel and her family.

"I'll call you as soon as I can." Adam threw him his wallet from the console. "Take out a few dollars for breakfast and lunch, just in case I'm detained. I'll call Pastor Johnston and explain the situation. I'm sure he'll come and get you."

"I'd rather be with you. I've been with some rough guys before."

"Don't even go there, Bud. Do me a favor and pray."

"I will."

"And keep all this to yourself."

"Sure. You can count on me."

Adam pulled into the front of the police station. "They know you're coming."

As soon as the door slammed shut, Adam took off. Granted, he would arrive at Archie and Thelma's farm after the police, but he needed to be there just in case Jimmy tried something stupid. Pushing aside the worst of scenarios, Adam sped through town and out into the country.

The clock in his car read nearly six-fifteen. The time had slipped by much faster than Adam anticipated. He strained to hear police sirens, but when nothing but silence met his ears, he envisioned they were already there—and hopefully everything was handled.

He searched the skies for signs of sunrise; even a trickle of light in the horizon would raise his spirits. Only blackness met his gaze, attributive of his mood. He prayed until sweat beaded his forehead.

Up ahead, flashing lights at the Myerses' place alerted his

senses. He counted four cars. Behind him, an ambulance sounded and flashed its lights. Adam swerved to the right for the vehicle to pass, then pressed on the accelerator.

"They have to be all right," he whispered. "They have to."

❧

Rachel sat with her parents and children in the living room while Jimmy paced the floor, wielding a pistol. In the lamplight, his reddened face indicated anger—out-of-control anger.

She sat on a sofa with her mother while Dad watched Jimmy. Autumn clung to Mom, who held Rocky. Summer had crawled into Rachel's lap. Mom looked ghastly pale. Her heart condition clawed at Rachel's heart.

"Your daughter's stupid." Jimmy waved the weapon in Dad's face. "I told her yesterday what would happen if she went to anyone. Stupid, really stupid. She called the cops."

"I didn't phone them," Rachel said more quietly than she would have thought possible, given the upheaval inside her. "They must have followed me."

"Liar. Why did you come out here?" Jimmy asked.

"To warn my family."

"Another stupid move on your part. I told you I was watching everything you did. Sure glad I crawled into the back of your car last night." He chuckled. "You might have outsmarted me."

Another flashing light shone through the living-room window. In the next instant, a siren pierced the air.

"How many cops do they have out there now?" Jimmy peered for only a moment. "Oh, so now they have an ambulance ready to cart off your bodies."

"Please, my children don't need to hear this." Rachel willed her heart to slow its incessant drumming. How could she think, reason, when her ears roared with the sound of her own terror?

"You always were stupid when it came to those kids." Jimmy wiped his face. "Slade, don't bring that stuff in here. Slade, don't talk to those kids that way. Slade, you're gonna

waken 'em up. You were always whining about something."
He pointed toward the window. "How about telling those
cops to get out of here before I lose my temper?"

"They won't go away now."

"Mr. Baldwin, come on out with your hands up. Let those
people go," a voice called from a bullhorn.

Jimmy opened the front door far enough to speak. "Fat
chance. I want fifty thousand dollars and a car in two hours.
Maybe then I'll see about letting these people go. In the
meantime, keep your distance or I'll start shooting."

"We'll see what we can do," blared throughout the house.

Jimmy slammed the door.

"I have to go to the bathroom." Rocky squirmed. "Real bad."

"Me too," Summer said. "I've had to go since we had to
get up."

"Forget it," Jimmy said.

"What's wrong with you?" Mom fanned herself. "Do you
want that mess here?"

"They're children," Rachel said. A plan began to form in
her mind. "Let Autumn take them. She wasn't able to go to
the bathroom when she got up either."

"Oh, you mean the pretty little thing with the loud mouth?"
Jimmy sneered.

"Yes, let her take them."

Autumn shook her head and clung to her grandmother.
"I–I'll be fine." Huge tears pooled her eyes.

"Scared of me, are you?" Jimmy asked. "Then listen up.
You take those two to do their business, then get back fast."

Autumn's lips quivered. Rachel slid from the sofa to the
floor and faced her daughter. She held her face in her hands.
"You can do this, Autumn. Simply go with Summer and
Rocky to Grandma and Grandpa's bathroom." Then Rachel
mouthed, *Go through the window.* "Can you do this?"

"Yes, Ma'am," Autumn said through wide-eyed horror.

"Don't waste any time." Rachel stared directly into the little girl's face, then kissed her cheek.

The children trailed to their grandparents' bedroom. Rachel wondered if Jimmy could hear the noise of the children raising the window—especially if it fell, as it had a tendency to do.

"What are you going to do with all that money?" Rachel asked. "You know the cops are going to catch you."

Jimmy glared at her, the way she remembered from days gone by. "I have a plan. I've dodged them before, and I will again."

"I know one time you didn't." She hoped to make him angrier, raise his voice.

"Rachel," her dad said. "Hush."

"She's stupid enough to make me pull the trigger," Jimmy said. "Too bad I don't have your boyfriend here and his kid. This would make a nice family reunion."

Her mother stiffened. Rachel didn't want to know what Mom was thinking. "He's not my boyfriend, Jimmy. He's my lawyer, and the boy is his nephew."

"You sure looked cozy walking home from work every night. Bet you had no idea I was watchin'." Jimmy paced the room like a military leader stating his strategy.

Rachel forced a laugh. "You are the reason he was there."

"I'm no fool. You two have something going on."

Jimmy's implication angered her. Controlling her temper took all of her might. "He's a fine man. Of course, you have no idea what that means."

"Rachel," Mom said. "For once listen to your father and be quiet."

"Why? It's only a matter of time before the cops burst through the door and unload their guns on him." She prayed her cocky attitude didn't get her killed, but the children came first.

"Where's those kids?" Jimmy asked. "They should have been back by now."

"I'll check on them," Rachel said.

Jimmy stepped forward and slapped Rachel, sending her reeling back into the sofa. Dad started to stand, but Jimmy waved the gun in his face.

"You stay there, old man." Jimmy swung his attention to Mom. She leaned over Rachel and wiped the blood dripping from her mouth. A tear dropped onto Mom's wrinkled cheek.

"You go check on those kids," Jimmy said, pulling Mom from the sofa. "And don't be all day."

Mom rose from the sofa and said nothing. The lines in her face indicated the fright tearing through her body.

Mom, go on out the window too. Please, your heart can't take much more. Another thought occurred to Rachel. The police could crawl through the window too. They could be in the house this very minute.

"Go ahead, Mom," Rachel said. "I'm okay."

Her mother hurried to her bedroom, calling for Autumn as she went.

"Bring 'em here now." Jimmy took a look out the window and smashed his gun through the glass. "My patience is wearing—" He peered closer and cursed. "Those kids got out." He whirled around at Rachel and lifted his gun.

A shot cracked, and Jimmy grabbed his right arm. Blood flowed between his fingers. Rachel heard her mother scream. Dad lunged at Rachel and knocked her down. Three policemen rushed into the room and wrestled Jimmy to the floor.

In the next moment, the house swarmed with policemen.

"Are you all right?" Dad asked, rolling from on top of her. "Did I hurt you?"

Rachel trembled. She realized now that the danger had passed, her body could react to the terror. "I think I'm okay."

Mom bent and wrapped her arms around her. "My sweet Rachel. I had no idea what you'd told Autumn until I saw they were gone. You deliberately made that man angry so he wouldn't bother the children."

"You would have done the same," Rachel said. "We're moms, remember?"

"We can't ever drift so far apart again," Mom said through her tears. "And I know it was my fault."

"I played a big role. How could you trust me? You had the

children's welfare in mind."

Mom held her for awhile longer until a policeman asked if Rachel needed a paramedic. Her face stung, and she imagined the imprint of Jimmy's hand looked worse than the actual damage. "I'd like an ice pack," she said, "after I see my children." She struggled to her feet and, with the aid of her parents made her way outside. Dawn had crept in unnoticed, and from the look of the clear morning, the day promised sunshine. Standing next to a police car were her precious children. Rachel stooped to her knees. Summer ran to her immediately and Rocky followed close behind, but Autumn snuggled into Mom's dress and the comfort of her arms.

Rachel saw the truth in her oldest daughter's quest for comfort. It hurt beyond any pain Jimmy could have caused. "You all were so brave," she said, not wanting to let go of Summer or Rocky. "And Autumn was the bravest because she ignored the danger and did exactly as I asked her."

"She's like her mother."

Rachel glanced up and saw Adam. He smiled, and she longed to rush into his arms and tell him how much she loved him. He bent beside her, and she leaned her head on his shoulder. So much she wanted to say to him and her precious babies, yet the words refused to come. Closing her eyes, she etched this moment in her heart forever.

"He can't hurt you again," Adam whispered. "You're free to live out your dreams."

Rachel stole a glimpse at her mother still clinging to Autumn and back to Summer and Rocky. She knew what must be done.

eighteen

"You can't be serious." Adam leaned against the side of Rachel's car. She held an ice pack against the side of her face where Jimmy had hit her. The children were safely inside the house. "You're exhausted. After you've rested, you'll feel differently."

"Rest? I have to be at work in less than two hours. This morning proved to me that my children belong with their grandparents. I nearly got them all killed."

"Correction. You were influential in making sure the police apprehended Jimmy. You've wavered with this custody hearing all along." He raked his fingers through his hair. "If I didn't think your children belonged with you, I wouldn't be your attorney."

"You don't understand. I'm playing with their future. I have nothing to offer them."

"But love and the role model of a godly woman," Adam said.

Rachel adjusted the straps of her shoulder purse. "I have to get to the restaurant."

"Honey, how can you go to work looking like that? A doctor needs to look at your face. Take the day off. Besides, the police will want to question you."

She turned her attention to one of the police cars pulling away with Jimmy. "Brenham's finest can't pay my bills. A little makeup and I'll look fine."

"Do you want a mirror?"

Rachel closed her eyes. "Whose side are you on?"

"Yours, always yours." He motioned behind her. "Here comes an officer."

The policeman strode up beside her. "Ma'am, we need you to come to the station and answer a few questions for us."

She glanced at Adam, then back to the officer. "Do you

have any idea how long this will take? I'm supposed to be at work by ten-thirty."

"Ma'am, I can't guarantee you'd be finished by then, and I suggest you make a stop at the emergency room. Your face is swelling."

"My face is fine."

At least she heard the advice from someone besides me. "I'll call Joan," Adam said. He gave the officer his attention. "Can I drive her to the police station?"

"Certainly." He nodded and stepped away.

"My car—" she began.

"Your dad said he'd take care of getting it back to town."

Rachel didn't speak to Adam all the way to the police station. He called Bud and reassured the boy that everyone was safe, and the police now had Jimmy Baldwin on his way back to jail. When the silence in the car grew unbearable, Adam talked about how well the police had handled the situation, her courageous role, and the tender manner in which her mother had treated her. No response. His chatting about reconciliation with her mother and children began to annoy even him—which meant Rachel was probably ready to nail shut his mouth. She stared out the window of his car. Her impassive stance sunk Adam deeper into confusion.

❧

Rachel finished at the police station and visited the emergency room of the hospital despite her protests, causing her to miss two hours of work. The X-rays showed no broken bones, and the doctor prescribed ice for the swelling. Newspaper reporters met her outside the hospital, shouting questions, snapping pictures, and sticking microphones in her face.

"Ms. Morton is not available for interviews," Adam said. Although she wanted to be left alone, having him around made her feel secure.

Once in his car and en route to her apartment, Adam attempted to make conversation again.

"Adam, I know you mean well, but I don't feel like talking. I'm not trying to steer myself into a pity-party corner. I need to focus on what God wants of me."

"I'm sorry. I'd like to walk you home from work tonight, even if Jimmy has been apprehended."

Rachel bit her tongue to keep from screaming at him. She didn't need a baby-sitter any longer. Swinging her gaze his way, she saw his earnest effort. "I'm fine alone, but if you feel it's necessary, then I'll see you around ten-fifteen."

"I'll be there too," Bud said. "I know I wouldn't want to walk home at night after this morning."

"See, you have two able-bodied men who want to protect you." Adam smiled and fought the overwhelming urge to reveal his heart.

Once at her apartment, Adam and Bud waited while she dressed for work and applied extra makeup over the left side of her bruised face and enlarged lip. The physical injuries did not compare with the pain piercing her heart over Autumn's rejection—and what she believed God wanted her to do.

The decision to again abandon the custody suit made her more depressed than she had been back when she'd learned she would have to serve time in prison. Then she had hope, a God who loved her, and a future with Him leading the way. Rachel attempted to reason with her dejection by repeating to herself that she had God and He'd never leave her. She hadn't been created to mother children but to glorify God. How she handled the situation displayed her Christian obedience. Backing away from the hearing sounded noble, holy. So why did she feel so miserable?

Wait-staff and customers eyed Rachel's face with a mixture of distaste and curiosity. She had no desire to explain the matter. Besides, the ordeal was none of their business; the newspaper would give them a full accounting tomorrow. Only Joan knew the truth, and she'd heard the story from Adam.

"Rachel, go home. This job isn't worth it," Joan said in her familiar motherly fashion.

Rachel poured glasses with water and placed them on a tray. "I'll go home if you feel my face is a distraction. I understand a battered waitress doesn't do much for business."

"It's not what happened to you. It's the weariness adding years to your pretty face."

"I'd rather stay. If I go home, then I'll be thinking about it all the time."

"I imagine so," Joan said. "Working does offer a better alternative."

Dad phoned shortly after lunch to find out when he could visit. Rachel told him around three, when the restaurant had a lull before the dinner crowd. She looked forward to seeing him. His comforting arms this morning had wrapped a blanket of love around her.

Shortly after the designated hour, Dad walked in with Autumn. The little girl's eyes were red and swollen. Rachel held back the urge to find out the problem. The hurt of so many rejections marched across her mind. Not today. She simply couldn't handle one more measure of pain from Autumn. Despite Rachel's wall of defense, she couldn't keep her attention off the child.

"Can we have a few minutes?" Dad asked. "Some place quiet where we can talk? Autumn needs to say a few things."

Rachel shivered at the implication of his words. From the tone in his voice and Autumn's tears, this must be a request to drop the custody hearing. "I've decided to stop the court proceedings," she said. "After this morning, I know the children are better off with you and Mom."

"Honey, that's what Autumn wants to talk about." He placed his hands on the little girl's shoulders.

"Okay." Rachel's reply sounded weak, beaten, and she knew it. She pointed to a deserted corner. "We can sit there."

Once seated in a booth directly across from Autumn with her dad beside the little girl, Rachel waited for one of them to speak.

"Go ahead, Autumn. Your mom doesn't have much time," Dad said. "Do you want me to leave you two alone?"

Autumn swiped at a tear. "No, Grandpa. I need you to help me."

Rachel handed her a napkin. How could one little person

pull out such fragile emotions?

"I'm sorry, Mommy," Autumn finally said. "I've been very mean to you." Tears spilled over her cheeks. "I've been ugly to you for a long time."

Rachel gazed into the reddened face of the little girl she loved more than life. "I believe you had good reasons."

"The Bible says I'm supposed to honor you, and I've never done it."

"You were angry, hurt at what I'd done to you."

Autumn shook her head. "I didn't think you loved me or Summer or Rocky. You were gone for a long time, and Grandma said you had important business with the State of Texas."

Rachel crossed her legs, rubbed her palms—anything to keep from breaking into a puddle. Her daughter deserved to know the truth. "Sweetheart, I was in jail for breaking the law."

"I know. Grandma told me. Daddy forced you to do bad things."

Rachel reached across the table and placed Autumn's hand into hers. "I made bad choices and paid for them."

"I did the same thing. I never asked if you loved us. I thought you'd rather live by yourself than with us. Every time I said bad things to you, I felt awful, but it hurt awful to see you and think you didn't care."

"Oh, Autumn." Rachel slipped from the booth and drew the sobbing little girl into her arms. "I've always loved you." For several long moments, she stroked Autumn's hair, whispering words of love and tenderness.

"I realized today that you loved us when you tried to warn us about that man. I was so confused when I figured it out, then you told me to get Summer and Rocky out of the house."

"It's all over now." Rachel repeatedly swallowed the lump in her throat.

Autumn kissed her on the cheek, and the dam of pent-up emotions spilled over Rachel's cheeks. "Mommy, I want to live with you. I want us to be a family. I don't care if we don't have money. I want us to be happy. Don't give up. Grandma says God can do anything."

Rachel fought to maintain control. "All right, Sweetheart. If you want me to fight, then I will."

Autumn lifted her green gaze. "God helped us this morning, Mommy. He will again, but you have to fight real hard. That's what Grandma and Grandpa said this morning."

Rachel glanced at her dad, but the words refused to come. His eyes were misty, and he swallowed hard. "Me and your mom thought you best hear this from Autumn."

"Thank you," Rachel finally managed. "I'd fight a thousand Jimmy Baldwins for this one moment."

"Mommy, do you remember the song you used to sing for us when I was little? When we lived with Grandma and Grandpa before you had to go away?"

Rachel searched her mind. Back then, she made up songs for her children like most mothers handed out cookies. "Which one?"

Autumn sat up straight and lifted her chin. She blinked several times, then her soft voice flowed through Rachel like sweet honey:

"A mother's love is the kind of love
That no one can take away.
She falls. She fails. God picks her up
To try another day.

"Keep the faith oh trembling mother
Your laughter sings on high
You give. You weep. God sees your plight
And dries your weary eyes.

"Someday when the nest grows quiet and clean
When the cries for mommy cease
You'll stop. You'll hear. God's whispers sweet,
His blessings you'll receive."

Rachel willed her lips to move, but the words refused to

settle on her lips. At last, she whispered, "Sweetheart, you have a beautiful voice. How did you remember all the words?"

"It was easy. I can play it on the piano too. Just like you."

Rachel dried her eyes. If she lived to be a hundred years old, she'd never forget the sweet words of her precious Autumn.

Dad cleared his throat. "Your mom is waiting outside in the car. She wants to talk to you. Miss Joan has already given her permission." He patted Rachel's hand. "We'll be waiting inside, might even have one of those special cookies."

"All right." Rachel nodded and forced a shaky smile.

"Grandma says she hasn't been a good girl," Autumn said.

Dare she hope Mom wanted to start fresh too? The mere idea caused Rachel's insides to turn cartwheels. Somehow she managed to rise to her feet and make her way out the door.

Mom waved from the car parked next to the curb. She rolled down the window. Tears trickled down her pale cheeks.

"Sit a spell with me, Rachel, if you don't mind. Your mother has a few things to say."

Rachel walked to the driver's side, opened the car door, and slid onto the seat. Her thoughts raced. Oh, how she wanted to believe this conversation would be a beginning of a wonderful mother-daughter relationship. She wished she'd grabbed a tissue, for her nose ran faster than a leaky faucet.

Without a word, Mom pulled a tissue from a box setting on the console and handed it to her. "I came prepared."

Rachel smiled and blew her nose. "Thank you for bringing Autumn. I wish I could have taped her every word."

"You won't forget them. They're engraved in your heart." Tears flowed from Mom's eyes again. "I need to stop this or I won't get any of the things said I planned."

Glancing into her mother's face, Rachel saw the love that she'd long forgotten.

"I'm sorry, Rachel. This is very hard for me. I'm such a stubborn old woman, but God has finally gotten through. This morning I asked God to forgive me, and now I'm asking you. I've been cruel and downright mean—a real nightmare. I've lied to my grandchildren and led them to believe you didn't care. At the time, I thought it was for their best. I really thought Archie and I were the best parents for your children, but I was so wrong. How wrong of me to hurt you time and time again. I should have been overjoyed with your rehabilitation and commitment to God, but instead I wanted revenge for the past. Then when you risked your life to save the children—and me—well, it was a picture of love and compassion. I'm so ashamed."

Rachel handed her a tissue.

Mom offered a faint smile, then touched Rachel's cheek. "Please forgive me. If you will give me a chance, I'll be the Christian mother God expects of me."

Rachel reached for her mother and pulled her into her arms. They both sobbed. "Oh, Mom, I forgive you. Look at what I've put you through. You think you're stubborn, what about me? We're really alike, and maybe that's why God put us together."

Mom sniffed. "We could be a good team."

Rachel shook her head. "We *are* a good team. We simply had to negotiate who was the One in control."

"Truce?" Mom asked.

"Truce."

"Sweetheart, I will do everything I can to make sure you get your children back."

Rachel's heart pounded, and she pulled from her mother's embrace. "I thought I was ready to fight again. Now I'm sure of it."

❧

Adam and Bud drove to the farm to assess what work remained on the house. If Adam had been in the mood to dive into a project—inside or out—lots could have been accomplished in the spring-like temperatures. On the contrary, Adam wanted to sulk, pout, and sink further into depression, and he failed to find a reason for his moodiness except that Rachel had given up.

They bounced along in his old truck as the morning's happenings darted across his mind. Today should have given

Rachel a perk, not defeated her. Jimmy Baldwin faced prison for a long time. Rachel more than proved her devotion to her children; her mother had initiated reconciliation.

If he lived a thousand years, he'd never understand women. Sad realization hit him. With Rachel giving up on the custody hearing, then she'd surely given up on him too. Odd how he considered Rachel, Autumn, Summer, Rocky, and Bud a chance at having a family. How could a man ask for more?

"Uncle Adam," Bud said, nursing a Coke. "Why are you in a bad mood? Tired? You and Rachel not getting along?"

Adam slid him a sideways glance, his usual response to his precocious nephew. Rather than regurgitate his thoughts, he sipped on his coffee, spilling a generous portion on his jeans. "Ouch. That's hot." He sat the Styrofoam cup back into the cup holder.

"It's about Rachel," Bud said, then handed him one of the clean rags they planned to use at the house. "Only a woman can make a guy nuts."

Keeping his eyes on the road while soaking up the hot coffee on his jeans, Adam wondered where Bud had gathered so much information about women. Considering the boy's parents, maybe he'd pass on asking that question.

"Rachel is having a tough time," Adam said instead. "Jimmy shook her up."

"So she needs downtime to pull herself together?"

Adam chuckled and tucked the coffee-soaked rag behind his seat. "Yeah, you got it, Sport."

Bud flipped on the radio and punched the preprogrammed buttons to various stations—none of which Adam approved. "What did you ever do without me?"

Adam expelled a tired breath. "Frankly, I don't know."

At the farm, he still didn't feel like doing much but cleaning and estimating how much longer the project would take to complete. He remembered the previous day with Rachel. She'd seemed excited about his house while Jimmy's threats raged through her mind.

I'd been in orbit. Why couldn't she tell me? Rachel's response echoed back to him. Jimmy had threatened him and Bud too. To think she'd called him the crusader when her behavior reflected some of the characteristics of Joan of Arc. He thought again of her deep desire to have her children. Rachel Morton loved those kids; she'd have died today to protect them. Now was not the time to give up. Tonight, when he and Bud walked her home, he'd talk to her again. Meanwhile, he'd be praying for God's will in this whole mess.

Adam and Bud sat on the porch steps. Despite Adam's mood, the day sparkled with beauty.

"Were you serious about adopting me, not just having custody?" Bud asked.

Startled, Adam peered at the boy. "Yes. Are you having second thoughts about it?"

Bud picked up a stick and doodled in the dirt with it. "Not at all. I'd always dreamed about it. I wanted to make sure you hadn't changed your mind. I mean, I know what a guardian is, but adoption is serious stuff."

Moved by the boy's honesty, Adam swung his arm around Bud's shoulders. "This doesn't mean that you are to forget about your mom and dad. I love them, and you need to find a place in your heart for them too."

"Pastor Johnston said the same thing, and I'm working on it. When you told me Dad had gone to Florida and Mom to New York, I cried a little. I even prayed."

"You can't forgive them by yourself. This is a God-sized project." Adam paused for a moment. "Loving you is easy, Bud. Loving my brother and sister-in-law is another story. Without God leading the way, I'd be bitter against them."

Bud offered a tight-lipped smile. "That's what I like about you. You're honest. Sure glad I have your first name."

"I'm rather partial to Adam too. We're a great team—you and me."

"As soon as Rachel gets her head on straight, we'll make a great family."

nineteen

The end of Rachel's shift that night came none too soon. As weary and achy as she felt, the glimmer of hope from Autumn asking her to fight for custody felt like a soothing balm.

Autumn loved her. She didn't want Rachel to give up. And what made Rachel's spirit soar even higher was that her parents encouraged her to fight. Win or lose, she had a reason to take a stand for her children again, and she couldn't wait to tell Adam.

Hopefully, her attorney still counted her as a client, if she hadn't ruined it by wavering back and forth with the hearing. A twinge of fantasy danced around her. Adam Raeburn cared for her; he'd told her more than once. One day soon, she'd tell him her feelings.

Humming an old hymn, Rachel finished wiping down the tables. Peace like a river flowed through her veins. She wanted to believe her life had taken a turn upward, although she well knew troubles were a part of her existence. But at this moment, she felt true joy.

Adam and Bud should be arriving any minute. Never, absolutely never, would she grow tired of seeing Adam's smile. She dared not dwell on the matter, but Bud would make an excellent big brother for her children. Shaking her head to dispel the fanciful notion, Rachel blew out a candle on the table. In the next breath, she watched Adam and Bud wave from the front of the restaurant.

"I'll be right with you." She felt a bit giddy. A fluttering in her stomach betrayed her heart. Rachel gasped. The sensation made her feel like a sixteen year old. "Would you like something? A piece of pie or some blueberry cobbler?"

"No, thanks," Adam said. He looked to Bud, who also declined the offer.

Remorse washed over her like a cold shower. Adam

jammed his hands into his jeans pockets—which meant he had a bad case of nerves, and it was her fault. He had every right to be furious with her.

Yesterday, he'd acted like a kid when he gave her a tour of his farmhouse. Adam didn't need her approval on his home; he was near perfect, standing there searching for the right words to say. Of course, the poor man hadn't been told about Autumn's visit or this new surge of commitment to winning her case. She gathered up her tips and purchased two, huge oatmeal raisin cookies for her escorts. They could munch while she talked.

"Thanks for stopping in." She handed them their cookies. "Here's a tip for your taxi service."

Both of them grinned, and she saw for the first time how much the two looked incredibly alike. The same narrowed eyes and firm jaw. They'd pass for father and son, which would soon be the case.

Stepping into the darkness, the chilly night air surprised her—mainly because she'd felt warm inside all afternoon. Tomorrow or the next day might hit her like a twister, but tonight she'd enjoy the serenity.

"How much work did you get done at the farm?" she asked.

"A little cleaning, and we picked out paint colors for Bud's room." Adam sounded tired, probably frustrated.

"What color?"

"Actually two colors. We're going to texture his walls to make them rustic looking. Sort of a burnt orange or faded rust." He shrugged. "The man at the hardware store called it faux painting. Don't know how to explain it."

"It will be wonderful, I'm sure." She turned her attention to Bud. "What kind of theme are you planning for your room?"

He swallowed a bite of cookie before answering. That homage to manners amused her. "Can't decide between race cars or horses."

"Both can go fast," she said.

"You are in a great mood." Adam held a twinge of surprise in his voice.

"Surprised?"

"A bit. What happened?"

Rachel took a deep breath as a well of emotion swept through her. "Dad brought Autumn to see me."

"And it was good?"

"Perfect, Adam. She apologized for all of her past behavior. The poor child didn't think I loved her. All those months I was gone, she thought I'd simply left them at my parents."

"Praise God, Rachel. You told her the truth?"

"Yes, but Mom had already told her about prison. Anyway, we had one tearful reunion." Rachel took a moment to contain herself. "She asked me to fight for her, Summer, and Rocky."

Adam swung his arm around her waist and gave her a squeeze. "All right, we're back on the front lines. What did your dad say?"

"Aside from getting a little misty-eyed, he and Mom agree I should battle for custody."

"I feel like celebrating."

She felt the smile in his words. "That's why you have the cookies."

"Finally." Bud's comment sounded garbled with his mouth full. "Let's get this court thing over so you two can get married."

"Bud!" Rachel and Adam chimed at the same time.

Suddenly Rachel felt that, with Bud's comment, she could give a small token of her heart. "Let's take one step at a time."

Adam squeezed her waist again. That little flutter hit her like a charging bull.

&

Bud Raeburn was a hard act to follow that night. Adam could have dug a hole through the sidewalk when Bud mentioned marriage in front of Rachel. She, on the other hand, treated the matter as though they were talking about shopping for shoes.

The court date was only a week away. In a few short moments, Rachel would be at his office to see him. With the change in Archie and Thelma's attitude regarding custody, the judge should rule on the case without a trial.

Anna buzzed him. "Rachel is here."

Adam chuckled. "Send her in." He could hear the teasing

in his secretary's voice, not that he minded. This morning she asked him how he intended to survive once Rachel no longer needed legal assistance.

"She may always have need for a lawyer," he'd said. How he hoped those words were true. He'd seen the caring in Rachel's eyes and in the tone of her voice. Expectations of the months to come made him as hyper as a kid on sugar.

The door opened, and the object of his affections stepped inside. "Good morning, Sunshine," he said. "I think we need to stop meeting like this."

She slipped into a chair across from his desk and assumed a most Victorian pose. Her hair looked different. She'd let it grow out a bit, and the ends rolled against her face.

"And where would you prefer? A small, quaint restaurant?" she asked.

He leaned over the desk. "A deserted farmhouse a few miles out of town. I've heard the owner only comes on weekends."

"Sounds perfect."

"We can conduct business on the way," he said. Without giving his actions a second thought, he snatched up his keys. "Seriously, I want you to see paint colors, and the chips are at the house."

Within ten minutes, they were heading out of Brenham. Bluebonnets and Indian paintbrush pushed up through the green grasses, and a farmer bounced along on his tractor. As much as Adam wanted to enjoy the vivid signs of approaching spring, he needed to talk with Rachel about the hearing.

"Next Friday is the big day," he said. "With your parents' support, I believe we will win this case."

She flashed a smile. "I think so too. Child Protective Services have Mom and Dad's recommendations that the children be returned to me."

"The likelihood of this going to trial is minuscule."

Rachel shifted in her seat to face him. "I remember you said the judge decides this."

"Right. The hearing will last about two hours, but the good side is it may be the last time you'll be in this position."

"Then I'd have a few weeks before the apartment is available, but Mom and Dad invited me to move in at the farm until then."

He didn't want to think about Rachel and the children packed into an apartment. He had other plans, big plans that included all of them.

"I have an idea," he said, hoping his apprehension didn't show through. "Why don't all of you live at the farmhouse instead of an apartment?"

"You're confusing me. That house is yours and Bud's. He'd be one disappointed young man."

"Not if he was sharing the house with a mom, dad, and sisters and a brother."

She stiffened, and he wondered if he'd once again spoke too quickly. "Adam—"

"Let me finish. You and the kids could live until—"

"Adam."

He swung his attention her way.

"Your plans are beautiful, and I appreciate them." She toyed with a loose button on her sweater. "I'm grateful for all you've done, but a blended family can't survive without love."

Adam felt conviction grip his heart. He'd thought about everything but the most important part. "I'm sorry." He turned into the farm's driveway.

"I know you are." Her soft voice did little to appease his guilt. In fact, he felt worse. "I've said this before, and I'm saying it for the last time. My children and I are not charity cases. We don't need to be saved—Jesus has already taken care of that. I will not marry a man who does not love me and my children. Your logical mind might have convinced you otherwise, but it simply won't work."

"Rachel, I do love you."

She startled. "Why haven't you ever said it before?"

"I forgot."

Her eyes widened. "You forgot? Is this like forgetting a form or forgetting to file a notarized document? You forgot?" Her green eyes flashed little gold sparks of fire, and he was on the receiving end. "Let me educate you. Love is the glue that keeps two people together. It's not the ribbon on the package, but the gift inside."

"What?" He couldn't follow her.

She opened the car door and slid out. With a wiggle of her shoulders, she marched to the back of the house. Adam cringed. He'd left a pile of trash there last Saturday, plus he and Bud had demolished the old outhouse—not exactly a choice setting for making amends to the woman he loved. He needed flowers, chocolates, and a carefully thought out proposal.

Adam palmed his hand against his forehead. Why hadn't he told her he loved her? He assumed she knew how he felt; why else would he talk about a permanent arrangement?

The bar exam hadn't prepared him for this.

He opened the car door and jogged to catch up. "Rachel, we need to talk. Hold up a minute."

"What about?" She didn't bother to swing her attention his way.

"You and me."

"There's nothing to discuss."

He walked in step with her. "I'm a fool, Rachel. I'm so sorry."

"That's nice." She crossed her arms and stared at the pile of debris. Bending, she picked up a rusty nail. "Somebody steps on this, and you have a suit on your hands."

"Very funny."

"You have your hands in your pockets. Of course you always do when you're nervous," she said.

Adam immediately withdrew his hands. "I'm not nervous."

She smiled and walked farther out into the yard toward the mass of rubble that was once a working outhouse. Stopping in front of it, she pointed. "Is this what I think it is?"

"Uh, probably. Bud and I tore it down."

She peered at it from a safe distance. "I suggest a nice flower garden."

Frustration had gotten the best of him. Long steps found him at her side again. This time he took her hand and dropped to one knee. "Rachel, I love you. I love you with my whole heart, and I've been an idiot not to tell you sooner. I don't want to think of life without you, Autumn, Summer, and Rocky. Will you please marry me? Will you rescue this lovesick man from his misery by saying yes?"

She tilted her head and stared at him. "Adam, are you asking me to be your wife at the site of an outhouse?"

Adam glanced at the wooden remains. "Yes, I am."

She bent down on both knees to face him. First she smiled. Then she laughed. "Tell me again why I should marry you."

"Because I love you."

"I'll need to hear those words every day for the rest of our lives, and so will our four children."

"I promise."

Rachel nodded at the remains beside her. "Will you plant me a flower garden there?"

"I promise."

"Planting something beautiful over the site of something ugly tells me you are willing to accept the good with the bad. I do accept your proposal, but first I have a confession."

Adam held his breath.

"I love you, Adam Raeburn. You are the only man who has made my stomach flutter, my heart turn flips, and my blood pressure soar beyond the safety zone. I want to look at you when we are old and feel a million times more than I do this very minute." She touched her hand to his cheek. "I promise to love you as God has instructed a wife to love her husband."

"God will always be the center of our marriage." He stood and pulled her to face him. Without another word, he lightly kissed her. She tasted warm and sweet, just like he anticipated.

Once he released her, she laid her head against his chest. Rachel giggled.

"What's so funny?" He held her tighter.

"Oh, can you imagine telling Bud that you proposed to me in front of the outhouse?"

Adam chuckled. "Can you imagine telling your children where you agreed to be my wife?"

"We're a pair, Adam."

"For a lifetime."

twenty

On the morning of the hearing, thunder roared and lightning split the sky in jagged bolts of white. As optimistic as Rachel wanted to feel, the weather left a dismal chill on her heart. She and Adam had prayed with Pastor Johnston the night before, and while those prayers had filled her with peace, she'd allowed trepidation to steal her joy.

Adam reached across the car and took her hand. "Today is in God's hands. He knows our hearts, and He knows you and I will provide a good home for the children."

"I know. I'm scared—afraid some unknown factor will sway the judge." She sighed and tried to smile. "I'm so glad I have you with me. If the best happens, we'll celebrate. If the worst happens, we'll cry together."

"You bet."

She glanced out the window. "This hearing is more terrifying than any ordeal with Jimmy."

"Talk to me, Rachel."

She hesitated. "You have no idea how heartbreaking it was to leave my children and go to prison. Rocky screamed and held out his little arms to me. Mom held him and tried to comfort him, but he beat his little fists into her chest. I guess he knew that I'd be gone for a long time. Summer and Autumn clung to each other like lost lambs, sobbing and crying for me. 'Mommy, Mommy' echoed in my mind until I wanted to snatch them all up and run."

Rachel crossed her arms over her chest. "It was horrible. Every night I went to sleep praying for my babies. Every morning I woke with the same nightmare—seeing them on that last morning, hearing their cries. Mom and I wrote back and forth, and she'd send snapshots." Rachel smiled. "My children colored pictures and Autumn would write letters. Then the letters came less frequently until they dwindled down to nothing at all. I assumed my children thought I'd abandoned them, and my parents had given up."

She rubbed her arms. "The days went on endlessly. I knew the truth, but there was nothing I could do. I prayed. I cried. I followed the rules and talked to others about Jesus, but deep inside I ached. . .still do."

"I'm so sorry," Adam whispered.

Her shoulders lifted and fell with a sigh. "I'm eaten up with regret and guilt. The word *shame* does not even touch the surface of what I'm feeling." She blinked back a tear. "Those feelings are not supposed to come from God. He loves me and He forgives me, but in moments like this, I'm overwhelmed."

"Keep praying, Honey. God is with us."

"I'm not looking for sympathy here. I made poor choices and I paid for them. I simply want you to know how much this hearing means to me."

Adam neared the courthouse. "We're ready to present the case. The outcome is up to God."

As she walked up the courthouse steps, she looked around for signs of her parents, her witnesses, or the caseworker. At least the children were spared this battle. When she saw no one, she wondered for a moment if Mom and Dad had changed their minds.

"Archie and Thelma are probably inside," Adam said, as though reading her thoughts. "And your dad assured me yesterday that they notified their lawyer of no longer needing representation."

Her legs seemed to feel like concrete blocks. Somehow, she put one foot in front of the other. Her heart thumped like a scared rabbit—such a strange sensation to want her children so badly yet fear the process at the same time.

"I love you," Adam said.

His words poured over her like a lullaby. "I love you too."

Inside the courtroom, her parents sat alone. Relieved, she

nearly cried. They both stood when she walked in. Dad hugged her first.

"It will all be over soon," he said.

Mom kissed her cheek. She'd been crying. "I love you, Honey. This will be okay."

Behind Mom and Dad sat her parole officer, a representative of Children's Protective Services, a court-appointed psychologist, Joan, and Pastor Johnston. All were there on Rachel's behalf. As though in a daze, she greeted each person and took her seat near the front with Adam.

The judge arrived twenty minutes later than the scheduled hearing. She hoped his arrival didn't coincide with the way he viewed her case.

Adam handled the legality of her case so expertly. To think this man loved her and wanted her children. God had given her a small miracle in the form of a three-piece black suit and matching wingtips.

"Your Honor, I'd like to call Joan Taylor to the stand," Adam said.

Joan's round face smiled in Rachel's direction, reassuring her.

Adam established Joan's relationship to Rachel, then continued. "How long have you known Rachel Morton?"

"Nearly ten months. She applied for a job at my restaurant the same day she arrived back in Brenham."

"How do you know this?"

"On her application she stated her release date from prison."

"What kind of an employee is Mrs. Morton?"

"I'd be lost without her. She always works two shifts and sometimes three. That means there are days she arrives at the restaurant around five-thirty in the morning and doesn't leave until ten or after that night. She's absolutely dependable. I rely on her heavily. She manages the restaurant as well as I do."

"Does she ever talk about her children?"

"Yes, Sir. They are the reason she works so much. She told me she puts every extra penny of her tips in the bank so when she receives custody, there would be money to help with expenses."

"Thank you, Mrs. Taylor."

Next Adam called her parole officer to the stand. The woman reported Rachel had done all the things required of her and had never missed an appointment.

The woman from Children's Protective Services sat stiffly in the witness's chair. Not a smile broke her stone-hard features.

"Would you tell the court about the last meeting you had with Autumn, Summer, and Rocky Morton?" Adam asked.

The woman nodded slowly as though forming her words. "I visited the children at their grandparents' home. As usual, they were spotless and well behaved. The home is clean, and the children are healthy."

"Thank you. Can you tell me what happened with Mr. and Mrs. Myers?"

"Both stated they had seen a significant change in Rachel Morton over the past several months. They said she was responsible, loving, and they recommended the children be returned to her."

The child psychologist reported Autumn had exhibited hostility toward her mother until recently, when she announced her desire to live with her mother.

"What prompted the change in the child?" Adam asked.

"An incident where Rachel Morton attempted to stop a man from hurting the children and the grandparents. Until that time, Autumn doubted her mother's love."

"And now?"

"She is convinced her mother loves her."

Pastor Johnston took the stand next.

"I have counseled Rachel since her release from prison—actually since before her sentencing. She is an active member of Brenham Community Church and a fine woman. I've seen her a few times with her children, and she has displayed a patient and loving attitude."

Archie and Thelma took the stand and under oath told how their daughter had gone from a self-centered woman to one of compassion.

The judge adjusted his glasses. Not a trace of emotion creased his wrinkled brow. "Rachel Morton, would you approach the bench please?"

Fear ripped through her. Did he have information about her that deterred him from awarding her custody?

"Mrs. Morton, I have seen and heard your efforts to be a productive citizen. Now, I want to know how you plan to take care of your children, should they be returned to your care."

She took a deep breath and willed her knees to stop shaking. "Your Honor, I plan to keep my current job but only work three nights a week. I have enrolled at the junior college to begin classes in the fall. I'll take six hours to begin with and attend on my afternoon break."

"Where will you live?"

Rachel glanced back at Adam. Mom and Dad didn't know about the proposal.

"Sir, I plan to get married."

Her mother gasped, and Rachel swung her attention to where her parents sat. Dad's face paled.

"Your Honor," Adam said. "May I approach the bench?"

"Permission granted."

Adam stood alongside her. Her breaths came in short spurts.

"I have asked Rachel Morton to be my wife. If the judge awards her custody of the children, I plan to adopt them as my own. I have a five-bedroom home in the country for all of us. Rachel and the children could live at the home until we are married."

The judge leaned back in his chair. He stared at Rachel and Adam for what seemed like forever.

"Mrs. Morton, what role do you see for your parents in the event I return the children to your care?"

A lump in her throat threatened to head to her stomach. "I want my parents to always have a close relationship with my children. I want them to feel free to have them overnight and to visit us whenever they wish. They have done an excellent job raising them when I didn't have the proper skills."

"I see." He read over the documents and forms before him. "With the information presented to me, I see no reason why Rachel Morton should be denied custody of her children. I hereby grant that Autumn, Summer, and Rocky Morton be returned to the care of their mother."

Rachel's head whirled. For a moment she feared fainting. A faint "thank you" escaped her lips. Adam grabbed her before she fell. He supported her waist and led her to the chair.

"Thank You, Jesus," he whispered.

Too numb, too elated to believe her ears, she could only hug this beloved man who had worked with her through the worst time of her life. They'd made a journey together, and a new path lay ahead.

God had answered her prayers. She had a new beginning—her precious three children, a twelve-year-old, soon-to-be son, a new relationship with her parents, and the love of a man God intended to be with her for the rest of her life.

God was good.

epilogue

Three months later

"Mommy, Mommy, come look," Rocky said. Dirt covered him from head to toe, the remains trailing across the utility room floor. "Hurry, Mommy, Daddy wants you to see."

Rachel hurried to the back door with Autumn and Summer at her heels. Bud, Rocky, and Adam had been involved in a "man-type" project all morning. She'd been given strict orders not to come outside or look out the rear windows.

Rachel saw a huge, oval flowerbed where an outhouse once rested. The men in her family had lined the plot with two layers of flat stone. Dark, cedar-smelling mulch oozed from between the stones, but in the middle sat clusters of daisies, miniature rose bushes, marigolds, periwinkles, zinnias, and other flowers that she did not recognize. Each type had been planted according to size and color.

"It's beautiful." She laughed. "And my men planted this all by themselves."

"Oh, it was a group project," Adam said. "Your parents kept you busy last night looking at the honeymoon pictures while we picked up everything we needed."

"You told me you were taking the kids for ice cream," she said.

"We did. Remember the chocolate stain on Rocky's shirt?" He winked and took a step forward to deposit a kiss on her lips. "How does it feel to be married two whole weeks?"

"Absolutely wonderful. But you didn't have to do this."

"I gave my word, and I saw how much it meant to you— the symbolism."

Rachel glanced at the four grinning children who watched

in wide-eyed wonder and then rested her gaze on her beloved husband. "One of the reasons I love you is the way you always think of others before yourself. You are the best, Adam Raeburn."

"And I'm married to the best, and I am the father of the best. What do you think of that?"

"I love you, Mr. Raeburn."

"And I love you, Mrs. Raeburn."

A Letter To Our Readers

Dear Reader:

In order that we might better contribute to your reading enjoyment, we would appreciate your taking a few minutes to respond to the following questions. We welcome your comments and read each form and letter we receive. When completed, please return to the following:

Fiction Editor
Heartsong Presents
PO Box 719
Uhrichsville, Ohio 44683

1. Did you enjoy reading *Compassion's Charm* by DiAnn Mills?
   ☐ Very much! I would like to see more books by this author!
   ☐ Moderately. I would have enjoyed it more if

   _____

   _____

   _____

2. Are you a member of **Heartsong Presents**? ☐ Yes ☐ No
   If no, where did you purchase this book? _____

   _____

3. How would you rate, on a scale from 1 (poor) to 5 (superior),
   the cover design? _____

4. On a scale from 1 (poor) to 10 (superior), please rate the
   following elements.

   ____ Heroine   ____ Plot
   ____ Hero   ____ Inspirational theme
   ____ Setting   ____ Secondary characters

5. These characters were special because?_____
_____
_____

6. How has this book inspired your life?_____
_____
_____

7. What settings would you like to see covered in future
   Heartsong Presents books? _____
_____
_____

8. What are some inspirational themes you would like to see
   treated in future books? _____
_____
_____

9. Would you be interested in reading other **Heartsong
   Presents** titles? ❏ Yes ❏ No

10. Please check your age range:
    ❏ Under 18   ❏ 18-24
    ❏ 25-34   ❏ 35-45
    ❏ 46-55   ❏ Over 55

Name_____
Occupation _____
Address _____
City_____ State_____ Zip_____

Presents